To Jean

R.H. Pearly

# LADY DALSWORTH'S
# DILEMMA

# Lady Dalsworth's Dilemma

Ralph H. Reesby

The Book Guild Ltd.
Sussex, England

The Book Guild Limited
Temple House
25 High Street
Lewes, Sussex

First published 1992
© Ralph H. Reesby 1992

Set in Baskerville

Typesetting by Dataset
St Leonards-on-Sea, Sussex

Printed in Great Britain by
Antony Rowe Ltd
Chippenham, Wiltshire

A catalogue record for this book is
available from the British Library

ISBN 0 86332 759 1

*To*
*My wife*
*Dearest Eugenie*

# 1

Lady Ursula Dalsworth was seated at the drawing-room window, where she could observe her son Clarence, busy building a small artistic bridge near the lake in the park which surrounded their home, Lynton Hall. Her brows were furrowed in perplexity as she reflected on her life these last three years since she had lost her husband.

He was a tall, handsome man as was her son, now aged twenty-five and so much like him, reminding her of her younger days. She was diminutive, yet at fifty-five years of age still retained the beauty, now more mature than that which had first attracted her husband while he was employed at the India Office in London.

Their acquaintance was of a short duration, for he was almost immediately transferred to India, where he soon made rapid progress and subsequently after three years returned to England. They again resumed courtship and eventually married in the private chapel of the Dalsworths in Lynton Park. Immediately after the wedding he had to return to India alone, having been offered a higher position in the Under Secretary's office.

Although the sudden departure of the groom was something which was accepted in those days as a cross which had to be borne by an empire builder, nevertheless it was a period of her life which could have been saddened more so but for the interest of Lynton Hall and the park, which his widowed father Lord Dalsworth had maintained in such splendour.

The Hall was immaculate, for his Lordship had served in the Indian Army and his treatment of the servants was similar to the regulations which he had applied to his junior officers.

Not that he was a martinet, far from it. He was a kindly man who engaged in so much activity that he was never lonely.

The young bride accepted the fact that her husband would be sending for her soon, while in the meantime she found plenty of interest here. She enjoyed horse-riding and would on occasion join the hunt which would often meet in the park. She was never in at the kill but her love of riding overcame her scruples, in her utter dislike of the final act. Frequently she would go into the village of Notley to see her aunt, who had looked after her since the death of her parents, for she had been only ten years old when she was orphaned and her aunt had been so kind that their mutual affection had done much to keep up her spirits. It was as a spirited young girl she had first met her husband at an open-air meeting of a local organisation which had arranged a flower show and gymkhana in aid of old pit ponies. Later when she was invited into the Hall and the ballroom she felt like Cinderella, but in her case she had fallen in love with the ballroom more than Clarence Dalsworth.

Now, as she sat looking across the park at his son who bore his name, she knew she could never recapture those times again; for since the death of her father-in-law when she had inherited the title of Lady, so many strange events had taken place that she felt it was time she did as her son was doing in the park by making a few changes in the Hall. She did not stir at once for she had other things on her mind. She remembered their sudden departure from India. Why was her husband retired so early in his career, ten years before the recognised retirement age? He then used to be away often, spending more time in London, and also had strange men visiting him at Lynton Hall; until she had protested at some of the characters, who were so unlike the gentry who came in his father's time that she felt sure some of the servants were being unsettled by having to attend them.

He agreed in future to acquire a flat in London where he would keep all the records of his work, while in place of visits he would have a private line installed at the Hall so

8

he would do more business from home. Also he would manipulate his affairs so that in future nobody would be contacting him in person as they would not know who he was.

This reply did not impress her, but as time went by she could not help but notice his looks were changing from those of a man of integrity to one whose features began to acquire the look of a gambler. From time to time the telephone would ring in his private sanctum and it was on an occasion when the door was left open that she happened to be passing. As she stepped inside to take the call she was brushed aside by her husband who rushed into the room, ordering her out and locking the door before picking up the telephone. Later he apologised profusely for his uncouth behaviour, saying that if she were to hear the telephone ringing again not to pick it up. This was his only request for not having people visiting to whom she had objected. He wanted nobody who telephoned to know of his address.

Three years, since his death, that room had remained as he had last used it, but some of his papers which had been left in the bedroom she had read, realizing he had amassed a huge fortune by employing others to defraud banks and insurance companies. His methods were so unusual, even the payments he made to his fellow conspirators puzzled her, until she had discovered the whereabouts of the flat in London which she visited and discovered every facet of his activities. The whole jigsaw was so clever that she had been tempted to emulate his actions, only to get the shock of her life by nearly ruining her and her son. She shuddered even now as she realized how stupid she had been, and all for a whim, but never again. No, she must get that den in her home cleared. It must not remain a sanctuary for crime. The private telephone had been removed some time ago and now she would clean up the room.

She paused from her reflections, glancing again at her son in the distance working with two other men in lifting a wooden beam. How he was enjoying himself in the park, which he had vowed he would make even more spectacular by planting unusual trees and shrubs. She pressed the bell at her side and her most trusted servant, Olive, appeared as she always did, immediately like a geni. She was more of a companion than a lady's maid.

'Olive, I have been thinking. It is three years now and I feel we should make an effort to clear the den, don't you agree?'

'Yes, ma'am, I do. I was only saying to Rosie the other day we . . .'

'Yes, yes, now listen, Olive, you can both start tomorrow morning and I will see what we can use the room for. Yes, that's it, thank you, Olive.'

Olive took her departure as Clarence, seeing his mother at the window on his approach to the house, came in through the French windows in response to his mother's beckoning hand. Clarence entered looking very hot and perspiring freely.

'Oh, Clarence, you must not tire yourself so. You have men to help you. Promise me you will not do all the hard work.'

'No, all right, mother, you should not have seen me in this condition. I was just about to have a quick splash and take the lads some drink. However, now that I am here, what is it you want, mother?'

'Well, dear, I'm having your father's den cleaned up tomorrow and I was wondering what use we can put it to. Anyway, I will not keep you now, you certainly look as if you could do with more than a splash, and I am certain your helpers need a drink.'

'That's all right, mother dear. Yes, you get the room ready and I can tell you now what I would like it for – a billiard room.'

Clarence quickly disappeared from the window, leaving a muddy footprint inside. Lady Ursula Dalsworth smiled as at long last a decision had been made and action taken. Nothing now remained but to see her wishes were made possible and a hoped-for period of tranquility would ensue.

Past events were going to leave those wishes deferred for a long time to come, for a legacy from her previous activities was about to bring considerable stress to both herself and her son Clarence.

☆ ☆ ☆

The following morning Clarence was again busy with his bridge in the park. Lady Dalsworth was seated as usual in her favourite chair in the conservatory, sipping the coffee which Olive had just brought in to her when Rose entered in a great hurry and almost incoherent as she gasped, 'Can you come at once, ma'am? It's the desk.'

Lady Dalsworth preceded Rose as they entered the den, to see Olive standing with a pistol in her hand which she was pointing at the desk. The scene was dramatic yet ludicrous, as Olive did not move and appeared to Lady Dalsworth as if frozen like a set piece on a stage. Meanwhile Rose had stepped back, taking up a position just outside the room. She recovered herself to say, 'We was clearing the desk, ma'am, when suddenly the side came open and the pistol fell out.'

'That's right,' said Olive, speaking for the first time.

'Yes, I know about the pistol, Olive. It is not loaded, although I think the master kept some bullets somewhere. He had it in India where he often kept it under his pillow; he retained it as a reminder of those days. It is quite harmless now. But I was not aware of any secret opening in the desk.'

Lady Dalsworth moved nearer and saw a roll of paper which she was able to reach in the secret compartment. Ascertaining that there was nothing else in the opening she pushed the side back quite easily and held the roll of paper up to the window to see written on the outside sheet, 'To my beloved wife Ursula.'

Olive was still holding the pistol in anything but a menacing manner until it was asked for, when it was raised pointedly at Lady Dalsworth before it was handed to her. Just as well it was not loaded, she thought as she instructed them to proceed with the cleaning while she retired to the drawing-room to examine the papers which seemed to burn her hand as she took her chair by the window. With trembling hands she undid the pink ribbon. Then, unrolling the papers upon which was her name written again, and much more in the handwriting of her late husband. Still very agitated at this message from

11

beyond the grave she drank the remainder of her coffee before commencing to read the narrative.

'My dearest wife,' she read, but had to wipe her eyes before proceeding:

I have placed this message in a place where it will remain until after my death; and I write with a very heavy heart at the disclosures which will cause you much unhappiness, yet ones which had to be told and ones which I was too much of a coward to speak of before.

I was always too aware of your beauty and your attraction to other men, that I knew my confession could so easily shock you into leaving my life forever. Therefore, my dear, when we were first married I was rushed off to India without even having time to perform my conjugal rights in any capacity which would have been adequate. A few fleeting nights together before my departure; and how I missed you. I knew you would be happy at Lynton, but I hoped and prayed you would miss me, perhaps if just a little bit.

My first six months were spent in the India Office in Delhi under the auspices of the Under Secretary, a post which in later years I hoped to adopt. It was while serving in this capacity that my immediate superior felt I should obtain some experience of the country and the people, but for safety I was to travel as a soldier with the rank of an officer in the Twenty-first Lancers. As you know my love of horses, it was just what I could have wished for after much office routine.

The summer months were extremely hot, so that when the regiment were ordered to go to the upper reaches of the Ganges, you will appreciate my willingness to become a voluntary unofficial soldier. It is not my place to speak of India, which you can read in any text-book on that country. However, I was intoxicated with everything I saw. Every new turn in the road brought an increase in colour and more glorious views as we climbed steadily towards the mountains. There was something romantic and yet remarkable in the various flowers and scents which seemed to change in grandeur at every turn through a range of hills.

We arrived one night at a small village named Patna

which was near the river bank. Here it was decided we should stay for six days to rest the horses; but it turned out we were to stay longer for there had been a heavy fall of snow in the mountains, with the result that we were cut off from further travel. The exceptional snow in these summer months was not predicted, neither the sudden thaw and the flooding which delayed our departure. I am mentioning this to give you a picture of the circumstances in which I found myself. We were unable to receive any communication from the outside world or even anywhere in India. So I could not get your letters, although I wrote to you in the hope that when communications were restored I could post a batch on to you. And now, my dear, I must tell you the story of my downfall.

We had been having a dinner at the officers' mess. Everything was very correct, but as the evening wore on, the drinks which were of a local brew started to take effect on some of the officers. I had only been drinking whisky but this was in very short supply for the reasons I have stated, and it appeared I was not keeping my place in retaining the honour of the regiment by refusing this home-brewed mixture. The officers, who had had more than was good for them, insisted I should not let the side down, and prevailed on me to just try the local brew. The result was, to put it mildly, a difference of opinion twixt that and the whisky I had already drunk, so that I was made very ill from the mixture.

The regimental doctor ordered me to remain in the hospital, which was a tent with four beds. I was alone until a day later my batman was brought in suffering from malaria fever which caused him to rave for two days and nights, which did nothing for my recovery. It was only when he became more noisy in his hallucinations that the doctor had him removed to another part of the camp. It was then my turn to get the fever. Also, three other soldiers joined me, two with malaria and another with a broken leg.

I must have started having deliriums, for I found I had been removed into a native hut where the doctor visited me saying my batman had died and the regiment would shortly be moving back to the plains. But I could not go as the drink I had consumed had worked as a poison which, coupled with the malaria, had rendered me too weak to travel. However, I should be left with two European soldiers and two Sepoys and hopefully I should be fit to travel in about a week. Tragically this was not to be, for no sooner had the regiment departed than the two soldiers were stricken with malaria, leaving only the Sepoys as my guardians. I now suffered another bout of sickness and was again delirious.

I thought you had travelled to India to me, only to learn afterwards that the Sepoys had called in a native woman to attend to my food and welfare. Strange how one's mind wanders to such an extent that one becomes certain of something which is only an illusion. One night the nurse had to hold me down, for in my imagination I thought I was dancing with you, dear, and then as we were both exhausted I felt you in my arms again, but this time quite passive; I must admit I committed the unpardonable sin in making love to a woman whom I thought was you, but in fact was the native woman. A few days later when I was recovering, one of the Sepoys told just what had been reported to him by the native nurse. He said he did not believe her story and she had been sent back to the village.

I realized now what had happened, but no good to my reputation would result from admitting to this charge; neither would anything be improved for her by this disclosure. Having fully recovered, as had the two European soldiers, we rejoined the regiment after three weeks' travel, eventually arriving back in Delhi where I was again able to read your letters which had accumulated. Mine in response from then on may have read differently as I struggled with my conscience in suppressing any statement which would disclose my unfaithfulness.

It was not until the spring of the following year that the Sepoy who had told me of the woman's accusation came to see me one evening as I was leaving my office, to tell me this native woman had given birth to a baby girl and she was white.

The shock was too much for me to hide and I knew as he narrowed his eyes that here I had to deal with a blackmailer if ever there was one. I turned away quickly to

14

a cupboard where I kept my whisky and asked him to sit down and join me in a drink; but I knew my fears were realized when he declined and at the same time said, 'I suppose there was no truth, sir, in her story?'

He was fully aware that it is an offence for a serving officer to have an affair with a native woman. On the other hand, I was not subject to military discipline, but a disclosure would be highly embarrassing.

I turned to him with my whisky in my hand, saying as flippantly as I could manage, 'Well, as you won't join me I'll drink to wet the baby's head alone.'

I do not think he understood my remark but I continued speaking quickly, saying, 'As you know, many soldiers were in the camp, held up by the snows, and such an accusation could be levelled against any European soldier, and the serviceman with the biggest pay packet would be the most likely one to be charged with being the father of the child; and an officer would just about fill that unenviable position.'

I emptied my glass as I was leaving. 'So, if that is all, perhaps things may turn out all right for them.'

I picked up my cane and we left together. He said no more except to give me a smart salute and a very clipped, 'Good night, sir.'

I went towards the officers' mess but turned aside to return to my own quarters to think how I could get out of this impasse; how to fulfil my obligations to the child, for mine I felt sure it must be; how to ward off a possible blackmailer. Yes, I had a lot to think about that night.

As I had explained to you, dear, although my position with the Under Secretary was good, my wages were still insufficient for me to save as much as I should have liked to prepare a place and give you the style of living that most of the ladies here enjoy. I was now more anxious than ever to have you here with me, and it was at this point of dreaming of our own home that an idea came to me as if in a flash of pure inspiration.

I had, amongst other of my duties, taken on the administration of a group of hospitals and was, as it were, a minister of supply. The supplies were ordered by the staff supervisor and I countersigned each consignment. I also knew of the patients who were admitted and discharged, and also mine was the final signature on the papers approving these facts. For some weeks I had automatically signed these items, but now I could arrange matters so that I could build up a surplus of supplies to our requirements and they would be available to be disposed of for cash to Indian private hospitals who were always complaining of shortages. In this I might be able to use my suspected blackmailer to good effect.

The supplies for the hospitals were calculated against the beds being used. While a new arrival would get a complete set of supplies, a resident patient would not. Therefore, I calculated that if I arranged for a few of the patients to go home for a short while, perhaps for a week – which many enjoyed – then I could have them re-admitted as new patients. I tried this idea out and found it could be accomplished without anybody being suspicious. I had arranged with the storekeeper to place the items on one side which were to be used for a future occasion. These were then removed to a building a little apart from the hospital. It had at one time been used as a mortuary, but had not been used for over a year as bodies were taken immediately to the other end of town.

The storekeeper felt he was sharing a secret with the British Government and myself against the possibility of a new war or a sudden pestilence. Of the items which were taken to the building, I had kept a strict record and carefully noted as any storekeeper. I had told him I was keeping records, to which he seemed greatly relieved at not having this extra work thrust on him.

It was while I was sitting and calculating my stock, late one evening in my office, that the Sepoy whom I suspected would be back arrived at the door. To his two knocks and my sharp 'come in', the door opened to reveal him in a state I would describe as not quite sober. I placed a glass of whisky before him which on this occasion he accepted.

'Well now, what can I do for you?' I remarked.

His eyes closed almost shut as he said, 'I understand you have got a lot of hospital supplies in the old mortuary. What do you intend to do with them?'

16

'You are a cheeky bounder, aren't you? I thought that knowledge was only for the British Government.'

I had previously arranged that he should become aware of this hoard. 'Yes there is a surplus there. It's against a contingency, although I cannot for the life of me see what.'

'I know,' he commenced, 'who that white girl's father is.'

'So?' I remarked.

He looked at me with red bleary eyes, but I said no more.

'Yes, I know who her dad is.'

'So you have already said.'

'Well now, if it is who I think it is,' he again hesitated, 'they may need a bit of help.'

This was a new angle for me to consider. If he intended to blackmail me, and of this I was more than certain, then he was intending to act as a beneficiary to the offspring at the same time.

'In what way?'

He continued, 'I know you have got a lot of stuff in the mortuary and I know where I can place it, at a price.'

'So you do, do you? You realize it will be the end of your army service if you are found out? I agree there is a surplus stock and it is embarrassing to hold too much, but your proposal is not to our liking at all. I am going now so you must leave, and if you do not wish to get into trouble, mention your idea to nobody. Understand? Nobody.'

He rose unsteadily from his chair, leaning on the table, and said, 'Goodnight, sir.'

We both stood looking at each other, I motionless while he was swaying, endeavouring to stand up to me. I let a few moments pass before saying, 'You may come back tomorrow night, but sober.'

His eyes flashed as he got the message. 'Yes, shir,' he gasped as he stumbled out into the cool evening air.

I sat for another fifteen minutes before proceeding to my abode to sleep the sleep of one who had accomplished a clever piece of human study. From now on I felt my star would begin to rise.

The following evening my Sepoy arrived. This time he was sober and immediately wanted to know if I had a proposition for him. To his surprise I said yes, sit down, but on this occasion I did not offer him a drink. I at once told him what I wanted; that was for him to dispose of the surplus articles which I had in abundance at the mortuary.

I knew he had made tentative enquiries at some of the private hospitals and clinics in the district. So I told him he would obtain the orders and I would fix the prices.

'And what will my share be?' he asked, rather too quickly.

I just as sharply snapped back at him, 'Fifty per cent of the profit.'

His eyes, which were half-closed with a look of cunning, suddenly shot wide open at the thought of such a bargain. I added before he could answer, 'Remember, the pay is good. You can do this easily when not on duty. You will soon amass a tidy sum, but if you do not wish to do this I can soon find another, as my position is quite safe and you can do nothing to hurt me. Should you think to do so your source of income would cease, for no better proposition has ever been offered to you or is likely to come your way again. So what is your answer?'

'Yes, I will do it.'

'Good. In that case you can start the day after tomorrow. I have a lot to do before you commence.'

And so a connection was built up between the Sepoy and myself and money started to accumulate as he disposed of the goods while I endeavoured to keep stock coming in by manipulating the incoming and outgoing of hospital patients.

The Sepoy would report regularly, saying he was increasing his disposals to more private hospitals. I was not too concerned where the articles went as long as increasing amounts of rupees were being credited to my account. I knew he was making plenty and not recording all his profit, but on the other hand I had wholesale deals with traders of which he in his turn knew nothing.

Suddenly our little arrangement ceased when the Sepoy's regiment was ordered to the commandant at the garrison at Dhera Ismael Khan. It was here that my Sepoy was transferred to another force to collect revenue at Leiah, and while in the vicinity were attacked along with two hundred Moulton Horse with six light field guns. However, they were defeated in the action and the corps returned with the six field guns to Dhera Ismael Khan. My Sepoy was not amongst those to celebrate the victory as he had been shot in the skirmish and died on the return journey.

This news was received by me with a strange feeling of release from the strain of having my secret exposed. I had previously made arrangements with him that we should each leave wills in each other's favour. I was quite aware that he would think of a way for my 'accident' as our riches grew, and I was equally prepared that I would not be the first. This misfortune to him gave me the increased wealth that enabled you, dear, to the villa which you said you would never wish to leave, for it was where our son was born twelve months after the birth of the girl in the hills, for I was deeply conscious I had an obligation to the child whom I knew in my heart belonged to me. My dear, I felt this child should be given the help in life that she deserved, for in my delirium when the little girl was conceived, I was with you dear, believe me.

My Sepoy had arranged that the child was receiving an education which I was providing. He would not tell me where she was but I saw receipts for the amounts he said were the school fees.

I was never able to see the child or her mother. At the same time I felt I was living a life of deception by not acquainting you of these facts. But now I wish to wipe the slate clean, to use an old cliché. I must record all, that you may judge me to be a weak character who has tried to make retribution. But I must continue.

The Sepoy had told me that the mother had died but the girl had escaped the epidemic which was the cause of so many deaths in the village. I went up to the hills to try and find her but without success, for the Sepoy had done nothing to help me. It was not until three months after his death that I received a communication saying in future would I send cheques direct to the school at Cawnpore. I made enquiries and found this was a very good establishment. I wanted her to be brought up with all the same kindness and understanding to which she was entitled.

19

The same, my dear, as we were giving our son. I do not know what has happened to her since we have left India; but I hope my mistake of the past will not be a burden for any of the family, if I might be so bold as to include her.

They called her Angela on account of her fair hair and skin. The school where she was being educated when we left contained some of the children of high caste Indian families. The curriculum was very extensive, including the teaching of French and English languages. Other activities such as social etiquette and dancing were taught, while in the ample grounds there was room for horse riding. Tennis and cricket were acceptable activities for the young ladies, who were being prepared for life abroad in Indian embassies with their parents.

As you know, dear, Clarence was just eleven when we left India for good, and my arrangements at the hospital I was able to close satisfactorily on our departure while no suspicions were aroused over the amount of rupees I was able to change into sterling. Father had recently died so that it was naturally assumed that I had inherited wealth from his investments in India, which in fact was not the case.

I hope in your heart you will forgive me. Should you feel my indebtedness has not been absolved by my actions on behalf of the girl I know not how to ask you, but I would like to think you were able to see no harm befalls her. The private school in Cawnpore is where I last knew her to be. I arranged that she should carry my name. That is all I can say. So somewhere in India is a young woman one year older than Clarence by the name of Angela Dalsworth.

I can write no more, but to end with my blessing to yourself and our dear boy, Clarence, and to say: Forgive me, my love.    Clarence.

# 2

Lady Ursula Dalsworth sat staring at the final paragraph; she could hardly believe what she had been reading. It was as if it were a novel written by a complete stranger that had no part to play in her life. Yet she dared not ignore this story. It did concern her, and try as she might to dismiss her involvement, she knew in her heart she was involved and it was expected of her to enquire as to the well-being, if not the whereabouts, of this young woman.

Her husband had been a trickster, and yet he had feeling. When they came back to England and Lynton Hall on the death of his father he was for a long time very morose and unsociable. The boy, being away at a school near Maidenhead, was no company for him except at holiday times when they would all go out together for a picnic, sometimes visiting his old school at Saint Piriams on the Hill. But more often they spent their time at Virginia Water or along the banks of the Thames at Cliveden near Maidenhead. Her son, who was fond of fishing, received tuition from his father in the art of fly fishing, becoming quite expert in the process, and said that one day he would enlarge the lake at Lynton Park. As these thoughts brought her attention back to the present, she looked across the park where Clarence was still engaged in building the bridge. How happy he was. She hoped he would lose his gambling habit, which was probably a legacy from his father.

At twenty-five years of age he was quite a handsome young man who showed no interest in the opposite sex; perhaps he never would. This gave her mixed feelings, knowing she would not like to lose his total affection. At

21

the same time, the line of Dalsworths should be continued; it was her duty that this should be encouraged.

Her thoughts returned to the letter she had been reading. How would Clarence react to the idea that he had a sister, or was it a half-sister? She was never sure of these relationships.

The most important matter now was what she was prepared to do. No, she would not tell Clarence about the papers. She had already told Olive and Rose that these were confidential documents which on no account should be mentioned to anybody. She would do nothing about them for the present and without further hesitation placed them in the desk between the two windows and safely locked them away, along with the pistol.

For the next fortnight Lady Dalsworth found she had plenty to occupy her mind in Notley, where she presided at the Womens Institute, meeting old acquaintances and a new associate, the police superintendent's wife, who would visit her with her husband, a very likeable man. Clarence had taken pleasure in his company, both being good horsemen, and they would often ride in the park, practising jumps and sometimes a race back home.

It was not until one evening when the superintendent and his wife came to dinner that she decided what she would do. Clarence was fully engaged in his activities with his bridge, so would not miss her. Yes, she felt she had a duty to perform, so now was the time to announce it.

The superintendent had just finished one of his stories when there was a short silence before she announced, quite abruptly, 'I think I will go to India next week.'

Clarence was the first to speak. 'Mother, whatever gave you that idea?'

'Just a whim, dear. Just a whim.'

She felt the policeman's eyes concentrating on her. She hoped she was not colouring up at this lie as she continued to speak. 'Well dear, why not? You are busy, many people now are away on holiday, we shall not get many visitors, so I felt I would like to see the places again where we were all so utterly spoilt and selfish together. It will be nice to meet some of the old servants,' she finished lamely.

'That's all very well, mother, but it must be, yes, fifteen

years since we left. Many of them would have moved to other parts and I am sure some would be dead by now.'

The superintendent interrupted to announce that the natives did die young, or so he understood. He continued, 'Do you think it quite wise? Would you be travelling with a companion?'

'Well, no. I had thought of taking Olive with me. But no, I shall travel alone to again experience the thrill of being once more in India. Do you know, Jack,' she addressed the superintendent by his Christian name while his wife Joan looked on speechless at this sudden decision of her friend to leave. 'Do you know,' continued Lady Dalsworth, 'the attraction of this country is something which unless seen is unbelievable to the average European.'

'So I believe,' said the superintendent rather drily.

Lady Dalsworth, unabashed, proceeded, 'There is nothing in this country to compare. In the mountains there are tall majestic forests of pine, silver fir, spruce, cypress and cedar.' Lady Dalsworth paused to sip her coffee while the superintendent and his wife Joan exchanged glances.

Clarence noticed this as the superintendent, looking at his watch, remarked, 'Very interesting indeed. It so happens I shall be going to London next week on a refresher course and will be away for six weeks. How would you like Joan to accompany you? It would be a new experience for her at the same time. I am sure you would make excellent companions, as well as help Clarence to be less anxious of you travelling alone.'

'Not a bit of it,' replied Lady Dalsworth. 'I am quite used to dealing with Indians, as Clarence knows only too well. Oh no, I shall be quite all right. But thank you; so good of you to offer, and Joan will have plenty to attend to as vice president of our association of women. Perhaps I should not have glamorised the countryside of India so much. Joan would not appreciate it as I will. The heat is excessive, while the flies and mosquitoes are always on the look-out for fresh blood and can make life very uncomfortable for a newcomer. Although I have been away for some time, one does build up a resistance to these creatures so that they rarely attack an old stager.'

'Mother, please,' said Clarence. 'And not so much of the old stager. But mother is correct,' he continued as he turned to the superintendent. 'India can be rather trying if one is not used to it. No, I shall not worry and I shall have plenty to occupy myself with, as I hope soon to take delivery of a billiard table. So I can amuse myself when the weather is too bad for gardening.'

The superintendent looked at his watch while his wife sat looking straight ahead. 'Ah, ah, just as I thought. Time is on the wing and I have to finish some reports before turning in for the night. Come along, Joan my dear, and thank you again, Lady Ursula, for another interesting dinner party, and we wish you well on your journey to India. Where to start from, Gatwick or Heathrow?'

'I am not sure yet but I leave all the travelling arrangements to my boy. He can do no wrong when it comes to organising.'

'In that case, Joan and I wish you a safe journey and, we hope, a pleasant time and speedy return.'

Joan said, 'Good night, Ursula. I shall be anxious for your return but I shall do my best as vice president.'

As their car drew away, making that gritty sound on the gravel which always indicated the arrival or departure of a vehicle, Clarence looked across the table at his mother who had a far-away look, one which he had noticed on several occasions these last few days.

'Now, mother, what is all this about?'

Lady Dalsworth nodded her head. There was a moment's silence before she answered, saying, 'Yes, Clarence, you are entitled to know. The fact is a native woman has given birth to a girl sired by your father. It happened very early in our marriage before I went out to him in India. The child was five years old when her mother died, which was half the age when I was left an orphan. Your father left this information in a secret drawer in his desk and I have only recently become aware of it.

'This young woman, if she is still alive, would now be twenty-six years of age, and bears the name of Angela Dalsworth.

'Your father had never seen her, but as he had made

provision for her upbringing I feel it is essential for me to search for her and satisfy myself that this person, who it is said is fair-skinned, is your half-sister, in which case I will ask her to come back with me to live here.'

'If you approve of her, mother, I will be only too pleased to be her half-brother.'

'Well said, my dear. Then you are not shocked by what I have told you?'

'Not at all, mother, I'm a grown man now. Say no more about it, I will make arrangements for your trip to India, and bon voyage.'

Lady Dalsworth's arrival in India was one which caused her very mixed feelings as to the correctness of her approach in contacting this young lady. It was very likely she would be married but her thoughts did not dwell on this. The drive from the airport was along roads no longer familiar, but wide thoroughfares with central gardens of flowers of all descriptions, accompanied by the heady atmosphere of perfume which did much to recall personal memories.

She had arrived when India was in its most colourful season and she could not shake off the feeling that her visit was pre-ordained. Why had she undertaken this journey on her own? She was extremely capable of doing all that she had set herself to do, yet she had strong feelings that she must complete her enterprise quickly.

Her stay in the hotel in Delhi had been arranged for three days. Although the service was impeccable and the food of the highest order she still felt the urge to proceed to Cawnpore. Here again was an excellent hotel from which she was to conduct her search for the school where Angela, whom she had already adopted in her heart, was educated.

The heat seemed more oppressive than in Delhi and the ride in an open car was not the joy one would experience on a warm summer's day in England, for the sun was relentless in its search for any kind of metal to turn into a hotplate. She was compelled to sit holding her parasol and, steadying herself by clinging on to the cloth fabric of the seat, she dared not touch the door for fear of being burnt. The driver, who seemed to accelerate on every turn in the road, noticed no discomfiture. Eventually they arrived at the school, a large building built on similar lines to an English country house. The grounds were quite large, yet as she neared the building the unkempt gardens were a disappointment from what she had expected from the information supplied in her husband's papers.

Her driver opened the door of the car smartly enough, but from then on was more interested in examining the tyres. She approached the large open door and rang the pull-bell. It was only after three long rings that she could hear footsteps approaching from some distance inside the building. She turned to observe her driver, no longer interested in his tyres, resting in the little shade provided by the car, smoking a cigar.

She felt life was not treating her too unkindly when a sharp 'Yes' obliged her to turn and observe a slaternly-looking servant girl, to whom she apologised for her inattention. Recovering her composure, she enquired if there was a Miss Angela Dalsworth living there. The dark features screwed themselves up in thought as she tried to understand or remember, but it appeared both failed her as she muttered, 'You had better come in. I will find out.'

On entering she found herself in a large square hall, the furnishings of which were rich in every respect but sadly neglected. There was no sign of life in the place.

The invitation to sit down by the carelessly waved arm of the servant was not accepted, for the richly covered settee looked dingy with accumulated dust.

After about five minutes Lady Dalsworth heard more footsteps but these were in sharp contrast to others, being quick and light; she was pleased to see a European lady of undoubted culture. She was dressed in white and immediately invited her into a room to the left of the doorway. This, by contrast, was clean and tidy; fresh flowers stood in a vase on a round table by the window.

'I always have fresh flowers each day as they do not last in this heat.' Lady Dalsworth's glance of approval had been noticed.

The woman in white introduced herself as Matilda. She was about the same age as Lady Dalsworth, one might imagine, although possibly much younger – India's sun will fade all flowers at an early age, be they vegetable or animal.

'I have to tell you,' explained the woman in white, 'that this school is not the same now, since the British have left. We are no longer a place for the daughters of gentlefolk.

'Your Daughter, I understand, is Angela Dalsworth?'

Lady Dalsworth nodded her head so very slightly. Can one nod a lie, she wondered?

'Just as I thought; yes, Angela was here with my other girls so long ago, but now they have all grown up and left.

'They were such a merry group, they and my assistant teachers who have returned to their own countries. Two have gone back to France and three to your own country.'

Lady Dalsworth gave a start, for she had not mentioned where she was from.

This gesture was seen by the woman in white who was quick to respond by saying, 'Oh yes, we know all about you, and Angela would often say how she would like to have met you.

'Yes, Lady Dalsworth, I know she was your adopted daughter and I could never understand why you left India without taking her with you or even coming to see her.'

Lady Dalsworth put a handkerchief to her eyes. 'You are quite right. There were many reasons and I am sorry I misinformed you just now, but I have come here today to try and find her and it is my intention to atone for the lack of parental affection which was her due. All I hope and pray is that she is well. My greatest wish is that she will be willing to return to England with me to share with my son and me all that can be offered in our home.'

Lady Dalsworth was visibly overcome as she said, 'You were all she had, as a teacher and as a mother.'

'Yes, I'm afraid I had to mother quite a few of the girls who often were lonely while their parents were abroad.'

A feeling of mutual friendliness was beginning to grow as Lady Dalsworth said, 'Do you mind if I call you Matilda? And you please call me Ursula.'

Matilda replied, 'Why, most certainly, thank you. Now I can tell you, as far as I know, Angela is quite well but left the school some five years' ago and went to live in Quetta, where I visited her two years' ago. She has developed into a beautiful girl, or I should say young lady. She was the star of my little band at that period. All the girls were from excellent families and they would always call me Matey, which was quite complimentary really.

'We were strict in those days, when all teaching and learning was a pleasure, but now alas,' Matilda paused for a moment before continuing, 'now all is different. The Government wish their representation abroad to be more in keeping with the ideals and thoughts of the proletariat. They do not wish the teaching to be as before and have provided their own curriculum and teachers.

'Today is an open day. The building is open, but as nobody ever comes it is proclaimed a holiday so that the scholars and staff are all away. My turn of office will cease in six weeks' time when I shall be returning to Germany and my retirement. What will happen here then I cannot tell.'

Lady Dalsworth was very touched by this story, realizing how embittered Matilda must feel after her period of being the head of a good school, to see it run down to its present state. What a sad finish to her career.

They sat looking at each other for a moment until Lady Dalsworth enquired how she would be spending the time during her retirement. Would she have another interest?

'Oh yes, I have friends in Hamburg whose children I can teach in their homes. What you call in England, I believe, private practice. I have no relations so will keep myself occupied in what I know, but I shall not wish to accept too much for I fully intend to do other things, perhaps travel. I don't know yet, but it is rather exciting to think of these things.'

She continued to talk about herself until Lady Dalsworth interrupted her by a direct question. 'Do you know where Angela is now?'

Matilda hesitated, saying, 'I could not say, as it must be about a year ago since I –' Matilda was interrupted at this moment by the girl who had met Lady Dalsworth at the entrance.

The girl appeared carrying a huge tray which held not only the teapot and cups but two jugs of hot water and a selection of sandwiches, scones and cakes. This heavy tray she held quite effortlessly until invited to place it on a table near Matilda which was obviously the correct place for it, after which she retired as quietly from the room as she had entered it, closing the door without a sound.

Matilda said, 'That girl hardly ever speaks to me. I feel she resents me as a symbol of a class she disapproves of. But she insists on presenting to me, at this time of day, a tea party par excellence. Do you take lemon? I can assure you the sandwiches are fresh, and as you can see, the bread is very thin. This is her speciality.'

Lady Dalsworth was only too pleased to accept this hospitality and her thoughts about the girl servant softened as she realized the care which was taken in the preparation of this tea party.

Matilda, without further prompting, proceeded to speak of Angela.

'Yes, it was some time ago when I received a letter from her. She was staying in Dagshai in Simla. I have never been there but I understand it is a very fine district. The climate is such that it is used for recuperation and was extensively built up during the British period for their troops to stay during the summer months. The Indian Government have not thought fit to interfere with any arrangements which were made then, and even now more rich families are building their villas in that district.'

Lady Dalsworth felt she could get no further information which would prove useful in her search and was preparing to make her excuses to withdraw when she suddenly thought, could it be possible that there was a photograph of Angela on the premises? In that she was unsuccessful, as Matilda explained the Indian educational authorities had insisted that there should be no reminders of previous scholars left there. Matilda had therefore sent them all to Germany. Matilda did say Angela was tall, had fair hair and was one of the most attractive young ladies she had ever had in her care.

One thing Lady Dalsworth felt pleased about was the fact that Matilda also would be leaving this place in six weeks' time. Yet while she bade goodbye to Matilda, she now had mixed feelings as regards to her search for Angela who would now be twenty-six years of age, and most likely married. However, she would go to Simla so that in any event she would have done her duty.

The driver, on seeing them at the entrance, picked himself up, discarding an empty beer bottle into the flower bed in the process, before opening the car door for Lady Dalsworth to enter. The return journey to the hotel was even more hazardous as the driver used one hand on the steering while the other hung nonchalantly from the side of the car door, where the wind soon reduced a cigarette between his fingers to ashes, only to be replaced immediately by another.

The heat now was not quite so oppressive, but her discomfiture was in no way made less by the carefree attitude of the driver, so that she was extremely thankful when they arrived safely back at the hotel.

That evening she wrote home to her son, telling of her observations and trials. She included many items with which he was familiar, such as the flowers of the countryside, which he as a small boy had made it his main occupation to collect, which was no doubt the origin of his present interest in the gardens at Lynton Hall.

There had been severe storms raging between Cawnpore and Delhi and she was informed that the trains had been interrupted so that she had to spend three more days at her hotel before taking the long journey back to Delhi. It was a ride which she did not look forward to as by now so many people had been delayed on their travels. Although every kindness had been shown her in placing her in a reserved compartment where there was less congestion, she found the long journey both irksome and unpleasant, aggravated by a migraine from which she always suffered during stormy weather.

It was with great relief that she was able to recognise the familiar landscape as the train approached Delhi. Delhi was home to her as she saw the twinkling lights of the cottages in the distance, soon to be outshone by the new street lighting and windows gradually being illuminated in the modern blocks of flats. So many more buildings, and how different from the Delhi she had known.

A hot bath at the hotel in the room which had been hers previously revived her spirits considerably so that soon the journey in that unpleasant smoky train was soon forgotten.

However, she decided to stay another day in Delhi while making arrangements to find accommodation at Dagshai. In due course she arrived, after a much more enjoyable ride.

The hills around here were covered with rhododendrons and deodar trees, giving the air a refreshing perfume of cedar which was in sharp contrast to that of the plains; for she was now seven thousand feet higher, which accounted for the cooler air where there was no need for air conditioning – which was very noisy and never very satisfactory.

The hotel where she had arranged to stay was excellent. Now she was getting to where she hoped to find Angela; and somehow she felt herself wishing that the young lady had formed no serious attachments. After the evening dinner she went into the room reserved for reading and writing where she found a telephone directory. She had no sooner seated herself and turned the pages to the Ds when the name 'Dalsworth Angela, Music Teacher' seemed almost to lift itself from the page. A mist appeared before her eyes. She could hardly believe that her search was near its end. Yes, there it was, without a doubt. Angela was here. No, she would not telephone but, taking down the address, would visit her the very next morning.

ANGELA DALSWORTH. TEACHER OF MUSIC. The words were clearly painted on a board at the side of a gate leading to a cottage, perhaps built to the requirements of an English serviceman, but it was no longer in the condition one would expect if sufficient funds were available for its maintenance.

Lady Dalsworth walked the short distance to the door. The garden, she was pleased to notice, had been carefully tended.

No music could be heard as she knocked at the door, which was opened almost immediately to display one of the most beautiful persons she had ever seen. For a moment she was speechless until a soft yet clear voice with a slightly French accent asked, 'Can I be of assistance to you?'

31

Recovering, Lady Dalsworth asked, 'Are you Angela Dalsworth?'

'I am. Please come in.'

Never had Lady Dalsworth expected to meet with such a beautiful girl. She thought for one woman to acknowledge beauty in another was a supreme compliment. Yes, she had heard that remark before, but this young lady was also a Dalsworth.

'I am Lady Dalsworth,' she said, after they were seated in a small room in which a piano was placed in a most conspicuous position, leaving little room for other furniture, of which two chairs and small round table appeared to be the only other pieces.

'Yes, I was expecting you. You look tired. Can I get you anything?' Angela quickly rose from her chair, saying, 'I know, perhaps a cup of iced lemon tea.' She bent forward, kissing Lady Dalsworth on both cheeks before turning and leaving the room, walking as one who has been trained in deportment, to reappear a moment later with tea and biscuits.

'So you know who your father was?'

'Yes, I know.'

'But why did you not contact me?'

'Because I would not have known how I would have been received, and I was content to wait for whatever may have occurred. I knew if we were meant to meet, you would come to me.'

Angela smiled at Lady Dalsworth, saying, 'Now I have seen you I know I would not have been rejected.'

Her smile was not only from her lips, but from eyes of blue-grey which appeared to bestow a gift of friendship, which Lady Dalsworth felt it was a privilege to accept. Never had she met in all her social activities anyone who looked, spoke and walked with such grace.

To think that Matilda back in Cawnpore had cultivated such a jewel and yet to have her work unappreciated by the present government.

Lady Dalsworth recovered to enquire how had life been since leaving school. Angela gave a wry smile. 'Not too good, er . . .'

Lady Dalsworth noticed the hesitation. 'Please call me

32

Ursula, and I will call you Angela.'

Angela replied softly, 'Thank you, I should like that.'

Angela continued talking, saying that her mother had died when she was still a child and her father then looked after her for a while. It was then that she learnt that her name was Angela, for her mother called her 'darling' but after she died her father insisted she was only to be Angela. She was not aware of her father's name until she was taken to a school and into the care of the governess who was introduced to her as Aunt Matilda, and who in turn insisted from then on she should be on the register as Angela Dalsworth.

'That was the first time I had heard my father's name. The governess was an excellent teacher; all the girls liked her. We used to call her Matey behind her back because she was so friendly. Nobody could have wished for a better schooling. When I left the school at the age of eighteen, Matilda told me she had heard from my father, and that he had provided a place for me in the hills, and although money would be made for me to remain independent he nevertheless wished me to use whatever gifts I had acquired to help other less fortunate children in the district.

'As you may have noticed, my gift, I suppose, was playing the piano. I have only given one public perform-ance. It was some distance from here at Queta, where I was very surprised to see Matilda, who had travelled a long way to hear me. But I have been nowhere since then. I have been giving piano lessons to very many children, but have felt recently I should have to make a small charge as, owing to inflation, my allowance is insufficient.'

She spoke in a quiet, even voice which showed no hurt at her diminished income. 'Indeed,' she added quickly, 'I have so much to be thankful for, and now I have a new mother I feel so happy.' Her eyes moistened at the disclosures she had just revealed of her present position.

Lady Dalsworth realized that the condition of the property showed that Angela was now poor. She had arrived in time and hoped her proposal would be accepted, for pride might make her prefer her independ-ence. However, great care would have to be adopted in approaching a difficult question.

There was a short period of silence before Lady Dalsworth said, 'Do you think you could obtain another cup of tea for me, dear? This is a very distinctive flavour.'

'Yes, certainly, mother,' the answer came with a smile. 'The tea comes from the plantations on the hillside near here. It is all freshly made. That is why the flavour is unusual. Even after two hours in the refrigerator the taste is entirely different. Another thing in our favour is that it is plentiful.'

When Angela returned, Lady Dalsworth had made up her mind how she should broach the subject of leaving here and returning with her to England.

'Have you any friends in the district, dear?'

'That I have not, unless it is the children. But there are not so many of them now, for the cooler weather is about to set in and most families have returned. Others will soon be going back to the towns in the plains so that when winter sets in this could be considered a ghost town.'

'And you stay here then, Angela?'

'That is right. I thought I would leave last winter and go down into Delhi, but the rents have been so increased that I am afraid it will be another winter spent here again.'

She looked steadily ahead, no sign of self-pity. The statement was a clear expression of her position.

Lady Dalsworth now spoke with conviction. 'That, my dear Angela, need not be. I have come from England especially to ask you to return with me where you will find a home and friends of the character you have adopted. For you must remember you are half English and you would enjoy the world in which your father would wish to know your talents have not been wasted.'

Angela's eyes were full of gratitude as she placed her arms around Lady Dalsworth and said, 'Thank you, my dear new mother. I knew you would come for me.'

'Now,' said Lady Dalsworth, 'you will have your own apartment at my home and I will see that we have a music room prepared for you. Yes, I know, that is just what I shall do. I will phone my son Clarence. Oh yes, I have a son. He is, or was, my only child. He's a year younger than you, dear. I am sure you will get along famously together.

'Now, dear, I will go back to the Hotel Baber. You know it, I suppose?'

Angela nodded her head. She felt too emotional to try to speak.

'I have a lot to speak to Clarence about. How long will it take you, dear, to arrange to leave? Can we say three days?'

Angela thought that would be sufficient time. Her subdued, 'Yes, thank you,' was sufficient encouragement for Lady Dalsworth to say, 'I will be back tomorrow, dear, during the morning to help you with your arrangements. Then later you must come back with me to the hotel and stay for dinner.'

Angela was delighted to accept Lady Dalsworth's help and invitation to dinner at the Hotel Baber, which was the principal hotel in the town and which she had never entered. Lady Dalsworth was of great help in the morning and Angela marvelled at her very efficient manner. Later, she knew, she would have no problems with such capable hands to help her. As they entered the dining-room at the hotel that evening she felt completely relaxed. Angela was a little in front of Lady Dalsworth as they were being conducted to their table so that from several paces back she was aware of the interest which Angela was creating by her entrance. Heads turned as, following the head waiter, she neither looked left nor right but proceeded like a princess, completely unconscious of the interest she had aroused.

Lady Dalsworth felt a warm glow of satisfaction, knowing that she was also sharing in this mutual regard and admiration. Matilda had done her work well in producing a lady.

# 3

Clarence received his mother's request for him to make alterations for the construction of a music room. He had already taken delivery of a billiard table, which now sat in glorious solitude in the apartment that was once his father's private den. His mother's request, he knew from past experience, with its strict instructions as to what she required, was an order.

So now he had workmen altering part of the conservatory in order to make a space for his billiard table. Now he had made arrangements for a grand piano (it must be a white one) to be delivered on the date the den had been completely refurbished in white and gold; twenty-four white and gold chairs had been ordered, while white and gold curtains had to grace the long windows. A dais was to be made on which the piano was to be placed. He had received strict instructions as to the carpets and other fitments; all must be ready by the time his mother and half-sister arrived at Lynton Hall. Clarence knew his mother's success in organising was such that some adversaries had called her a manipulator.

Clarence was at Heathrow when the plane from India arrived. He first saw his mother and then Angela, who was a head taller, walking or rather gliding along beside her. She was everything her mother had described. One word he felt would have been sufficient, and that was elegant. He greeted his mother in the way an only son can, very, very affectionately. Then, turning to Angela, he said, 'Welcome sister. How nice you are.'

These words seemed so trite, yet he could think of no others. Angela smiled, saying, 'Thank you, the pleasure is not all yours.'

That night a dinner to which the superintendent and his wife were invited provided a most cordial home-coming, which was completed by Angela insisting on playing some of Chopin's Nocturnes in the new music room. It was her way of acknowledging all that had been done on her behalf.

Now she said, 'I am prepared to give free music lessons again. Thank you both Ursula, mother, and brother, Clarence, for this wonderful welcome to this beautiful home and heavenly music room which surpasses anything I could ever have dreamt would be possible; and even now I feel just as Cinderella must have felt as she waited for the clock to strike midnight.

'Thank you. I hope I shall be worthy of the name of Dalsworth. Your kindness is . . .' Angela's voice faltered. She could say no more.

The superintendent made a few remarks to cover everyone's embarrassment before the little impromptu concert ended.

Life at Lynton Hall changed considerably as it reverted back to the days of a previous era, which Lady Dalsworth remembered as a young bride when her father-in-law had provided so much entertainment and excitement at the Hall to keep her from fretting during her young husband's absence. He encouraged people in the village to use the ballroom and the Sussex Hunt were allowed to meet in the park, and this was just what was happening now. Angela and Clarence would join them, both being excellent riders. On other occasions all three would ride to the far end of the park where there was a brook which fed the lake and here they would have a picnic by the water's edge. Later they had a race back home which invariably was won by Lady Dalsworth, whose skill in encouraging whatever horse she rode made that animal develop more speed than any other rider was capable of accomplishing.

The evenings were often spent with Clarence trying his skill in the billiard room in which the superintendent would join him. Angela would be happily engaged with her piano playing in the white and gold music room.

On other occasions Lady Dalsworth would join them to

make up a four for a few games of bridge. The superintendent's wife, Joan, did not play bridge but enjoyed playing billiards, which was a game Angela did not like. While Clarence, in his turn, was not a music lover. Except for these differences, both brother and sister were happy together in most other pursuits.

Angela and Lady Dalsworth were spending quite a lot of time together. Both being musical they would go to London whenever there were concerts which they wished to attend, often staying several weeks, which they called their London season. These seasons often followed each other with very short intervals between.

It was during their absence that Clarence would endeavour to do the pruning and dismembering of old and decayed branches of the elms on the estate, which neither his mother nor Angela liked being performed while they were there; these necessary amputations were not to their liking at all. It was on such an occasion that Clarence went into the village to purchase rope required for the work.

After he had bought the rope and done a little more shopping he visited the local inn for lunch, where he found himself sitting next to an elderly man, whom he thought he had seen before when he and his men had been renewing fences knocked down by the huntsmen. They would invariably pay for the damage, which meant Clarence found that much of the fencing which was getting old was gradually being replaced by new and stronger stakes.

The old man said he was always interested in the home of the Dalsworths as it was where an old associate of his said he lived.

'I'm Clarence Dalsworth.'

'Yes, I know, sir. As I say, I was in India the same time as your dad. In those days we shared quite a lot of time together up country near the Himmalay district where one has to cross deep ravines, perhaps with only three ropes to hang on to, which would be swinging in the wind enough to tip you off if you weren't hanging on tightly. Your dad and me shared a lot of similar experiences together.'

Clarence felt this man was hankering after something, possibly a job. But as an old soldier, whom he thought he might well be as he had known his father, it would be polite to ask him what he did.

'Well now,' the old man remarked, 'I must admit I know very little except soldiering, and that's not much use in civvy life, but one thing I can do and that is masonry. I did that before I went into the army, where I was employed in rebuilding the old forts after we had knocked them down. Sometimes we had to do them up again after the moguls had had a go at them. Yes, I can dress a stone. There's not much in that line I can't manage.'

'How old are you?' enquired Clarence.

'Fifty-eight, sir, and still fighting fit. My father was mason at Canterbury Cathedral and he was still cutting stones at seventy-four.'

'Right, well now. Do you want work?'

'I do indeed, sir.'

'In that case I will be quite frank with you. I do need a mason to replace some of the coping at the Hall. Do you think you could manage heights?'

'Governor, when one has lived as long as I have in the Himmalay, he has no fear of heights. Yes, I could be your man.'

'Right, then,' replied Clarence, 'you can come and see me tomorrow at nine o'clock. You will find me in the harness room. I will leave a message in the servants' hall so that anybody you meet, tell them who you are and they will bring you along. What is your name?'

'Thomas Atkins, sir. No, don't smile, sir, that is my true name. I think that is why my old dad had me put in the army.'

'All right then, Thomas, until tomorrow.' Clarence finished his beer, said goodbye to the landlord and stepped into the bright sunshine, leaving Thomas to drink another pint to celebrate his good fortune and thinking to himself he knew how to make himself indispensible. He ordered another drink, enjoying the thought that it was no use acting an old soldier without knowing how to tell a good story.

Coping stones will be easy after replacing the rocks on a

fort. One can always replace coping stones and at the same time loosen others. Oh yes, he could keep that job going for a very long time.

Clarence found that Thomas was as good as his word. He was an excellent craftsman who, with another man he had provided in order to assist in raising the stones, soon made good progress on the roof, which it appeared was in a more dangerous state than Clarence realized. He now thanked his good fortune in meeting with an old soldier who knew his father, although his father was not in the army in the true sense as he was a civil servant assigned to the army to obtain administrative intelligence. However, Clarence was satisfied with the man's work and that was sufficient justification for keeping him in his employ.

Lady Dalsworth and Angela, having completed their London season, returned to Lynton Hall to find scaffolding near the entrance while a lot of new stones were lying nearby, ready to replace others which she could see were very old looking and worn from the effects of wind and rain. Lady Dalsworth decided there and then that she would have much more done to the building to give it a freshness which would be in keeping with the considerable amount of redecorating already completed inside. After she and Angela had taken some refreshments Angela retired to her room, while Lady Dalsworth started to look through her accumulation of letters. She knew very well that Angela would be absent for quite a while as she was giving a piano recital that evening to some of the women's guild and their husbands, which the superintendent and Joan would be attending.

Angela would always have a hot bath before these occasions and today, after the journey, she knew how this would relax her for the practice she always took beforehand.

Lady Dalsworth continued to read her letters until, after a while, she could hear the sound of small sketches from various composers which Angela was trying out in the music room. Picking up the next letter, which was face downwards, she was surprised on turning it to see that it had a German stamp affixed. She pursed her lips and frowned as she tried to recall any person who would be writing from Germany. The postmark Hamburg immediately brought to mind the identity of the writer. It could be none other than Matilda. She did not open it at once, but continued to look through the rest of the mail, leaving Matilda. She hoped it would be a pleasure deferred. The anticipation of reading this letter she likened to the enjoyment of the bouquet of wine when one hesitates before the tasting.

It was quite a while before Angela returned after having completed her preparations for the evening performance. When she did so she could not fail to notice the excited look on Lady Dalsworth's face as she held an unopened letter aloft, saying, 'Come and sit by me, my dear. I have received this from Hamburg, which if I am correct may be from Matilda, your old school governess.'

Angela sat down quickly. Her face had lost a little of its colour.

Lady Dalsworth, not noticing, continued to speak. 'Yes, that's right. Matilda told me she would be returning to Germany and in all probability it would be to Hamburg where she hoped to occupy herself taking private pupils.'

Angela recovered her composure as the flap of the letter was being lifted.

'Yes, it is from Matilda. I had given her my address.' She commenced to read aloud:

'Dear Lady Dalsworth,

Thank you for letting me know where you live, and I hope you were able to trace dear Angela. She is a jewel. I hope you are well and trust your journey to India was not wasted. I realize now I did have a letter from her saying she was teaching children to play the piano, but after your visit I had another of my old pupils come to see me – her name was Dorothy – who told me that Angela, who she had met at Dagshai, was very busy (Lady Dalsworth looked up from reading but Angela's face was turned away) and was settling down well. Now I can say the same, for I have found a very nice apartment which I have managed to buy. It is quite near a park and I can receive children here and give lessons just as if I were back in India.

'The weather is more to my liking also – none of the oppressive heat and the struggle to remain cool. But you

41

know all about that, so I will not bore you by speaking about the climate, in spite of which the country afforded me so many happy years with my girls which will remain a consolation for the rest of my days.

'But now, what about yourself? Did you manage to find Angela? I am perhaps presumptuous in writing to you, but my curiosity is because of the affection I feel for my star pupil, for whom I have always envisaged a life in society which would be far more comprehensive than that to be found in a Simla hill station.

'If you feel you can write to me my address is Flat 5, Bismark Rusterstrasse, 22 Hamburg 12 Postfach 110643. Should you do so, it is Fraulein Henkel, but Matilda to you, if you will pardon my forwardness on such a few moments of being in your company.

'My blessings, Yours sincerely,
Matilda.'

Lady Dalsworth placed the letter back in its envelope. 'Well now, Angela, what do you think?'

Angela turned to her with moist eyes. 'It is a very nice letter, Ursula. How kind of her to remember me.'

'Not only kind, my dear, but I think we owe her the information she seeks. I will write and ask her if she will be able to get free from her pupils for a while to come and spend a few weeks with us. Would you like that, Angela?'

'Oh, yes please. Do write; I should so love to see Matey Matilda again.'

'That is settled then. I will write first thing tomorrow morning.'

That evening the music seemed to be infused with a poetic spirit as Angela's hands seemed to float over the keyboard while her fingers caressed the notes which filled the music room with Chopin's immortal nocturnes.

Even Clarence, who attended, was affected by the atmosphere of concentration, as each one in that little party dreamed their fantasies as the music proceeded. The evening's entertainment finished with a promise from Lady Dalsworth that other evenings would be arranged when Angela would be playing a selection of Debussy, Ravel and Johann Strauss. And so ended another musical evening at Lynton Hall.

42

The next morning Lady Dalsworth's letter was sent to Matilda, who replied that she was pleased to know that Angela was with her and she herself would be delighted to accept the invitation. Her arrival two weeks' later at Lynton Hall provided a scene which she hardly expected, as both Angela and Lady Dalsworth came forward from the doorway to greet her, while Clarence was first to hold the car door open before the chauffeur could alight.

After dinner that evening Matilda spoke of her life in India and shared reminiscences with Angela, who was pleased to confirm the authenticity of some of the magical happenings which the fakirs would perform. Lady Dalsworth was quite aware of this from her own experiences but was content to remain silent while listening intently to those things which she had seen for herself many years previously. The retelling by another enhanced and re-called more vividly the scene, which in some parts she had forgotten completely.

Matilda's stories eventually brought her back to the present time, as she spoke of her present life in Germany which, after her long absence, had changed – so much crime now everywhere. She continued to speak of the present lack of moral behaviour, to which Lady Dalsworth was paying but very little attention until she mentioned a recent robbery from a security van in which twenty million dollars' worth of notes were taken as they were being transferred from one of the banks to the airport. The security van, which was heavily guarded with a following police escort, was nearing the airport and had to travel through a small wood when trees fell between the van and the escort, with the result that the van completely disappeared and was not found until three days' later when both the contents and the driver had vanished.

When Lady Dalsworth heard this she felt herself trembling, as this robbery was almost a copy of her own, which she in her stupidity had organised in order to imitate the clever manipulations of her late husband. Now, here was an exact enactment of her own ideas which she had hoped had been lost forever. Why should she have to suffer this all over again? Was another about to start a series of robberies which would ultimately reflect back to her?

When she had performed her foolish act she was fortunate at the restraint which had been imposed on all the press so that details of her involvement had never been disclosed.

This time it might well be that other journalists in Germany might seize on the likeness, which, when ventilated in the West German papers, would be eagerly reproduced in England. Matilda was still talking while these thoughts were going through Lady Dalsworth's head, then recovering she again heard Matilda, who was explaining that the money was thought to have been transferred into Switzerland, although the Swiss authorities had stated no large amounts of dollars had been deposited into their banks.

They did admit under pressure from the West German government that several deposits had been paid into different banks and that the amount had been calculated as similar to that which the West Germans were seeking. They were not prepared to disclose the owners of these accounts until such time that it could be established without any doubt that the money came from the robbery in West Germany. They would be willing to assist in any way and had, for the time being, frozen these accounts.

Matilda, having said all this, then repeated the sense of it again as she summarized the outcome of these events by saying, 'In my mind this was money from the robbery. Without any doubt it had been paid into banks under different names so that when all the interest in the robbery had subsided these accounts could be put into one or sent abroad.'

Matilda sat back in satisfaction at again being in congenial company. Each one in the group remained silent, until Angela asked Matilda, 'Why are you holding your face?'

'It's just a tooth, my dear. I should have had it attended to before I left, but I was so anxious to meet you both that I came without having it seen to.'

'In that case,' said Lady Dalsworth, 'you must visit my dentist in London. He is quite excellent. Angela went to him once but only saw his assistant, but he is very capable.'

Angela replied, 'Yes, he is very good. You will be quite safe in his hands.'

Lady Dalsworth continued, 'He was recommended by a Mr Nigel Danton, a barrister in London who has been here on two occasions.'

She suddenly stopped as she realized she had exposed herself to questions, which if asked would be very embarrassing for her to make any form of reply, for he was one of the enquiring agents who had found out about her own single venture into crime, on which the West German robbery seemed to have been patterned.

Matilda thanked her for her kind offer.

Clarence was speaking to Angela, so that the sudden cessation of words was not noticed. However, instinctively Angela felt that Lady Dalsworth had said something which she wished she had not. Lady Dalsworth quickly recovered, hoping the pause had not been noticed, saying, 'You will like him. He is German, coming from Frankfurt, and has been in this country many years; his English accent is real Oxford. I will telephone for an appointment tomorrow and we can have a day in London. Angela will not come with us as the London life has proved a little too hectic for her.'

'Quite right,' agreed Angela, 'I need a while in the country now, for London does seem closed in after the space of India, but I shall like it very much when I have had more experience.'

Early the next morning Angela was in the music room when Lady Dalsworth entered, saying, 'Just a few words with you, dear, if you are not too busy.'

Angela was not too busy and welcomed this visit which she felt sure was going to be about the offer of dentistry made to Matilda last night. Having seated themselves on the settee by the open window, Angela could tell that she was sitting by a very worried woman who was silent for a moment before starting to speak.

'I have been thinking about my talk to Matilda about the dentist last night and I feel you should know more about us here at Lynton Hall.

'Your father was a very clever man and when we came back from India I'm afraid his cleverness led him along paths which are only taken by crooks and cheats. I'm sorry to have to tell you this and I know it must hurt you deeply. I, having found some of his material, was also tempted to try my gambling instincts, for I always enjoyed a flutter on the horses; that was a weakness of mine, but no more. I was tempted at this stage to copy his method in what I thought would be a masterly accomplishment. However, things did not turn out well and that was the first and last time I have ever done anything of this nature. I was younger then and certainly most foolhardy in the extreme.

'When I spoke to Matilda last night and mentioned a dentist, I also said he was recommended to me by a Mr Nigel Danton. He was a private detective of a special nature, although in his ordinary capacity he was a barrister. He spent the war years in MI5. He is a very astute man, as you can tell, and is only invited by the government to undertake inquiries which would not be placed with the CID, and I am afraid I was placed in that category which only he was to investigate. It was he who could have exposed me if he had wished, but the case which I had so badly managed was settled out of court, if that is the right expression.

Now I have a very strong feeling that the robbery in West Germany which Matilda was describing, was so similar to the arrangements which I had employed that it might well be that I shall fall under suspicion as the one who is behind this present security van hold-up. I am quite aware that the British police know nothing of my own past naughtiness, but it is just possible that the German government could exert enough pressure on our government to cause my name to be mentioned.

'I said it was a very private inquiry in which I was concerned, and yet . . .' Lady Dalsworth hesitated before continuing, 'I would like you to know, dear, your brother Clarence knows nothing of what I have told you.'

Angela sat perfectly still, looking towards the piano. She gave no sign of having heard the last remark.

Lady Dalsworth remained silent for a moment, but as there was no reaction from Angela, she continued, 'Now Matilda, being German the same as the dentist, may, given the chance, become talkative and repeat to him the story of the German security van hold-up, in which case it is very likely the dentist will pass on this knowledge to Nigel Danton and if so he will at once connect this incident with me and Lynton Hall. You see, I am in a predicament and do not want inquiries here. It would be most embarrassing, don't you understand?'

Angela agreed, saying, 'I know a little from stories I have heard in India of daddy, and bear no ill-feeling. Indeed, why should I? He has left me provided for; while you, Ursula, have given me more love than I could ever have hoped for. It is my duty as a daughter to do all that is possible to protect my benefactress.'

'Well now, my dear, thank you for saying that, but what shall we do?'

They both sat silently for a while until Angela spoke very quietly and deliberately.

'The best way to prove our non-participation in the German robbery is to let this Mr Danton find out from us. We would wish him to exercise his skill so that he will discover that we are not the ones. Or rather you, Ursula, have to let him know in a devious way so that he will assume you do not wish him to think it is you who has given him this lead.'

'Yes, I follow you, dear. I think that is perfect. Now, how to go about it? Ah, now, let me see. Whether Matilda says anything or not, I think we should let Mr Danton know in as mysterious a way as possible, so this is what I suggest we do. I will write a letter, very short, telling him to phone a number which I have installed here; it is not in the telephone book. You, Angela, will answer, asking him if he has visited his dentist lately, or words to that effect.

'Now, if Matilda does speak to the dentist then I am fairly certain the dentist will inform our Mr Danton, who will then be curious to discover the origin of the voice which spoke to him on the telephone, and he being the clever one will have no difficulty in discovering it is mine. He will then think that I was trying to let him know about the German security robbery which was so much like the one I had arranged, about which he knows everything. He will come to the conclusion that I was informing him to

47

establish my complete innocence; he would understand my need for secrecy, so I hope will not make inquiries here in any official capacity at all.'

Angela had been nodding her head. 'Yes, that seems sound. If Matilda says nothing and the dentist does not contact Mr Danton, the letter you send and my telephoning will not amount to much, so will soon be forgotten.'

'Excellent summing up, my dear. Now I will send that letter off to Mr Nigel Danton so that he receives it before I take Matilda to the dentist.'

# 4

Nigel Danton was in his chambers at Lincoln's Inn Fields with his secretary, sorting the accumulation of mail, in spite of all his precautions to ensure that this would not be too burdensome for them after their return from the summer holidays. Now they were faced with the prospect of a full morning's work arranging the letters for replies. Nigel Danton felt and looked out of character for one who spent most of his days in the Law Courts or his own private chambers. For now his body had the tan produced by the sunny island of Cyprus where he had spent his vacation at the Amathus Beach Hotel.

Standing over six feet, he made an impressive figure at all times, but now with his tanned features, piercing grey eyes and dark hair he looked more like one's conception of a prosecuting counsel than one who habitually accepted the role of the defence.

Silence reigned in the office, to be broken only by the slicing of the envelopes and the occasional cough or gasp, sometimes a suppressed chuckle at one which called for no reply.

George, his secretary, was the first to speak, remarking, 'This is a funny shaped envelope,' which he held up for Nigel's inspection. It was diamond-shaped and also constructed of brown paper.

Nigel said, 'They will do anything to attract attention. What's in it, George?'

A quick movement with the knife found the envelope empty, but by laying the envelope completely flat only the bold inscription 'Telephone 458212' was printed on the inside.

'Is that all?' inquired Nigel. 'We will not bother about that one, then.'

They continued to sort the mail until George's pile had been accounted for. He was about to take these into his office for attention when the brown envelope caught his eye. 'What about this one?' he enquired of Nigel.

'Yes, all right, get it over with. Give it a ring.'

George did so and was asked by a very modulated feminine voice if he was Mr Nigel Danton. George replied, 'One moment, please.' Covering the mouthpiece he said, 'It's a lady by the sound of her voice, asking for you.'

Nigel took the phone. 'This is Nigel Danton. How can I serve you?'

A question was asked in a voice which seemed to purr as it asked, 'Have you visited your dentist lately?'

Nigel was taken aback at such a question. Had it been an ordinary voice he would have hung up the phone, but there was something very attractive in the lilt of the words which were very English but had the insinuating charm of the French dialect.

He found himself compelled to answer, 'No, I have had no occasion to do so.'

Nigel found himself anxiously awaiting the reply, and after a short while the same soft tone answered, 'I am sorry. Forgive me for disturbing you.'

Nigel was about to speak again when the telephone was replaced. 'I wonder what all that was about,' he said, speaking more to himself. He would have liked to continue listening to that dulcet voice. Replacing the telephone he continued with the correspondence until he came to a letter from his dentist asking him for an appointment. Now he was puzzled, looking straight ahead as George, without another word, went silently into the inner office.

Nigel was examining the history of a firm's accounts when George came in to say a messenger had come from the Home Office and wished to speak to him. He was known to them both and soon explained that Nigel was required to report at the Home Office as soon as he could. This arrangement was customary when he was required for special duties; the phone was never used. Nigel, without any hesitation, said he would be free tomorrow afternoon from two o'clock onwards. The time was convenient so that the following day Nigel found himself waiting with three other men in the appointments room at the Home Office. He could tell that the others were from Scotland Yard, having seen them there on previous occasions. They were called first, all departing at five minute intervals and being conducted by different ushers.

After a wait of twenty minutes since the last one had departed he was escorted to the fourth floor, where the Home Secretary was waiting to receive him.

'Nice to see you, Danton. Let me see, it's Nigel, isn't it?'

'Correct, sir.'

'Good. Right, we'll get down to cases straight away then, Nigel.'

'I have had a communication from our ambassador in West Germany who has been requested to enquire if the robbery of an armoured security van containing a considerable quantity of dollar notes has any resemblance to anything which may have occurred in this country. Now, as you know, Nigel, our efforts to track down the Manipulator were kept secret, and yet these particulars which they have given me of their robbery are identical to those employed by the Manipulator. Do they know anything? We did not have our security van robbery reported in any journals. Now we have this enquiry from West Germany it is obvious to me that we have to find if the Manipulator has started again. You know who I mean?'

Nigel nodded his head.

'I want you to look into things and find out if it is a crime perpetrated from that source or not. Let me know your findings. Now, if you wish to bring in your friend at this stage . . .'

He paused as Nigel volunteered, 'John Royston.'

'Ah yes, I know you were together in MI5 during Hitler's botheration. Anyway, I leave it to you to be discreet, that is all.'

Nigel now found himself committed to an enquiry he did not relish. He would phone John, who was the landlord of the White Horse Inn, situated in one of the most picturesque villages in the Cotswolds. Nigel did not give details over the phone, in accordance with the Home Secretary's explicit instructions. John's reply was to take the next train to London, to be met at the station by Nigel who took him directly to his club in Piccadilly.

That evening Nigel briefed John on the visit to the Home Secretary's office and what was required of them. He then spoke of the dentist's visit, the unusual letter, the voice of an angel as Nigel described the telephone words asking him if he had visited his dentist recently. John could not help but notice the change in Nigel's voice as this was recounted.

'Frankly, Nigel, I can make very little from what you have told me so far. Is the Manipulator in business again but operating in West Germany? The first thing, I imagine, is to find out where the telephone message came from. You had the number. Why didn't you ring up and enquire?'

'That I could not do, as it would immediately have put them on their guard.'

'Would that have mattered?'

'It certainly would have done. I looked for it in the directory and found it was ex.'

'So?'

'Don't be in such a hurry.' Nigel was a little peeved at John's abrupt words. He continued, 'I had no difficulty in discovering it came from Lynton Hall.'

'You sly old fox. Why did you not tell me at the outset? You're getting more introvert in your old age.'

'Thank you, John. Well, that is it. I wanted to find if your first line of approach was the same as mine. Now we know, but what to make of it defeats me.'

So the conversation continued until it was decided, just as Lady Dalsworth had anticipated, she would not be visited.

Nigel had agreed with John. Nothing could be achieved at this stage by an approach to Lynton. He felt, as Lady Dalsworth had anticipated, she was only trying to protect herself from unwelcome publicity. Yet Nigel was still intrigued by that voice and more anxious than ever to acquire the name of its owner.

Nigel's report to the Home Secretary on his next visit admitted he saw no connection between the robbery in West Germany and the similar previous hijacking of a security van here.

Life at Lynton Hall was good. Lady Dalsworth and Matilda had spent several days in London together. Matilda had received her treatment at the dentist, whom she found very satisfactory and with whom she was able to converse in her native tongue. Angela was still enjoying the country air, so reminiscent of life in the hills of Simla, while Clarence had found more work was required on the rooves of the Hall, the weak portions of which his mason was so adept at discovering.

They were gathered in the conservatory one afternoon when Matilda said she would have to return to Germany as she had some pupils who would shortly be coming back from their summer holidays; so she would have to be there, otherwise they would go elsewhere for their tuition. Lady Dalsworth noticed that Angela looked a little pensive at this announcement by her old mistress, who also noticed her expression and exchanged glances with Lady Dalsworth. She said. 'I have an idea.'

'Permit me to interrupt you, Ursula. I think I know what you have in mind. Now, Angela, how would you like to come back with me to my place in Hamburg? I have plenty of room for you, my dear. Also I have some very good friends who have an establishment in the country quite near. It is not so large as Lynton but they have quite extensive grounds and are keen on hunting, having some good horses which I know they would be pleased for you to ride. I have told them about you and they do have a grand piano so you could play to them. I know you will be very welcome after you have tired of my little abode in Hamburg.'

'Dear Matilda, I should not tire of your place, and if Ursula does not mind, it will be lovely to spend a while with you. And as for your friends, I shall be pleased to meet them, but never will I prefer their company to yours, and I shall only look forward to returning to Ursula, Clarence and my new home. You know, I think you two have been discussing me.'

'We have,' admitted Lady Dalsworth, 'and I can say I'm very pleased you will be accompanying Matilda. I have plenty to occupy my mind at the moment and I feel Matilda will be more of a companion than myself.'

When Clarence heard they were going back together he was delighted, as he explained he would be going to Frankfurt in about a month's time to take part in the horse trials there, and said if they were still in Hamburg he would like to go along and see them.

'Delighted,' said Matilda.

Angela also could only agree. Clarence then excused himself as he departed to the stables while his mother, saying she had some letters to write, went into her own miniature room which she called her studio. Not a single painting could be seen. She did not profess to being an artist, yet she would spend many hours in there writing. Others in the household thought she may have been writing her autobiography. But whatever it was, it was her closely guarded secret and she insisted on calling it a studio.

It was raining when Angela and Matilda arrived in Hamburg, and the evening was darker than normal. Matilda gave a little shiver as she entered the flat, saying, 'It's good to be back and we will soon warm ourselves after the journey. I did not like to say anything to you before, but I am sure we were being followed. I cannot give any reasons for this feeling, it was just a vibe which I seldom find is wrong.'

Angela said, 'Who would want to follow us, dear?'

'Perhaps you're right,' agreed Matilda. 'However, we both will feel better for a hot cup of tea.'

# 5

'West German Bank Security Van Robbery,' screamed the headline of the London Evening Clarion. Nigel Danton could not help but notice this as he entered the Piccadilly club. He had been having a particularly trying day and thought to seek relaxation in a game of billiards, but that, for the moment, was not to be. Calling for his customary whisky and soda he settled down in an easy corner seat to read the report of this latest robbery. He hardly touched his drink while reading how twelve million marks had been removed from a security van, so like the previous robbery in which the van itself was hijacked, and almost a carbon copy of this type of theft first attempted in the lanes of Kent. He had checked everything at Lynton Hall and had felt if he was again approached by the Home Secretary he could give him a detailed account of his investigations, although he was still unaware which of the visitors had that angel's voice.

He continued to meditate until a steward approached him saying there was a billiard table now available and a gentleman there wished to play. Thanking him, Nigel saw a person whom he had not met in the club before, but he gave Nigel a very good game and in fact beat him handsomely. Nigel's invitation to another game was not accepted as the other said he had another appointment. This answer seemed strange as Nigel had made no appointment to meet him.

'Thank you for the game, sir.'

The words were behind him as he was putting his cue in its rack. Turning quickly he found a card being proffered. As he took it, he noticed it was plain card. His winning adversary who had handed it to him had already reached the door as he read the other side. 'Please be at my office ten o'clock tomorrow morning.' It was signed Ronald Belmont. Nigel looked towards the door where the man was still waiting for a sign. Nigel gave a nod, holding the card from the private assistant of the Home Secretary.

Nigel knew directly he entered the office he was in for a rough time. He could hear the Home Secretary's voice through the half-opened door which in itself was something out of keeping with his particular penchant for privacy. Ronald Belmont, whose name was on the card, passed through from his own office without glancing towards Nigel. At last the call came.

'Come in,' boomed the voice of the Home Secretary. 'Come in, Danton.'

Nigel entered, closing the door behind him. If he was in for a dressing down he did not wish to share it with any outsiders.

'This is a pretty kettle of fish,' he commenced before they were seated. 'I've had another report from our ambassador who is having a rough time trying to convince the German authorities that we knew nothing about a Manipulator interfering with their security cars; I had to let him know of some of the things which happened here so that he could reply to their questions, but how they found out about our Manipulator bothers me.

'I have read your report, Nigel, and you feel Lady Dalsworth and her son are not involved in this latest escapade. But since your enquiries I have had observations made at Lynton Hall. You have been busy with your own affairs so you would be unaware that there has been a German woman visitor. Also a young lady from India who professes to being a daughter. Now, the facts are these: both these females have now left Lynton Hall and are at present staying in Hamburg where one of them has a flat. They have been there about a month. Also, two days ago the son went to Germany in connection with horses, to buy some probably, but one thing is patently clear – the Dalsworths were in Germany at the same time the robbery occurred. What can we make of that? Is it a coincidence or are they involved?'

Nigel did not answer. He was thinking. Was one of them the one with the angel voice?

'Well,' the Home Secretary's voice cut into his thoughts like a sudden crack of a whip. He had noticed Nigel's mind had been wandering, but now his attention had been recalled he continued.

'Our police at Notley have been alerted to the situation there and Jack Markham, our Super, has been to Lynton on several occasions. But except for him, I did not want the police to know too much because of the undertaking I gave to the Indian Government to play down any publicity after their rubies were held up by the Manipulator in Kent before they were due to appear at the Royal Academy. That's something which has given me nightmares, and is an experience which I do not intend to suffer again.'

He looked hard at Nigel as he added, 'Not if I can help it.' The Home Secretary now waited a moment or two before continuing.

'So, Nigel, to put it in a cocoa-nut, I want you to drop your work and resume your MI5 duties, if you think that is the right term. Both you and your friend Royston will be put back into service. This time I want you to report to room 243 at Scotland Yard where you will meet the Commissioner who is treating this business discreetly, as you yourself will do. Now, when can you start? To-morrow?'

'Not possible,' replied Nigel. 'I shall need tomorrow to farm out some of my more pressing problems, but I can promise the day after.'

'Good man. Then it will be 10 a.m., room 243. You do not contact me; all your business will be through the Yard where I will leave any messages that come my way which I consider will be helpful.'

The Home Secretary rose to his feet. At six feet three inches he seemed to tower above Nigel as he wished him goodbye. Nigel, on leaving the building, was filled with apprehension as to the correctness of his first report that all at Lynton Hall were in the clear.

Arriving back at his chambers he immediately tele-phoned John, telling him to report to room 243 at Scotland Yard the day after tomorrow, and he would meet him there. This sharp message was all that John required to realize that he had been recalled to special duties. Also that something had upset him. Nigel was usually rather frivolous in his speech and approach to life, but when a mood descended on him it was as a calm before a storm. When it broke, his actions, thoughts and speech moved with the speed of lightning. John knew by these signs that the job to be done was a big one. In the meantime, Nigel and George were busy distributing their work in every direction to ensure that George was not too harassed during Nigel's absence.

John and Nigel were seated in room 243. They were silently reading the manuscripts which had been provided for them to understand.

'This is going to prove a difficult nut to crack,' said John.

'What, the understanding or the job?' replied Nigel, whose mood had become sarcastic. Relenting just a little he qualified this remark by adding, 'The Home Secretary said it would be a cocoa-nut.'

The Commissioner was to have met them at ten o'clock but it was not until eleven that he appeared. He was not a particularly impressive man. His bulk made him seem shorter than he actually was; however, in expressing his apologies he smiled, giving them the feeling that he was a likeable man with whom they could co-operate.

'Have you read the reports, gentlemen?'

His voice was very light but his dark brown eyes were steady as he read the answer in their faces before their lips could utter one.

He continued, 'You have been given this assignment which will require you to travel to West Germany in furtherance of your enquiries which will lay the ghost of this affair and also please the Home Secretary.

"In the meantime we are keeping a low level here, only checking who's at home and when.'

At that moment the telephone on his desk rang; he answered, 'Yes, this is 243. Ah, yes, and how is he now? The doctor has been visiting him today. Oh, I see, he will be back tomorrow. He, umph, will, will he?'

The Commissioner's remarks were heard by both, and

especially by Nigel, who felt the Commissioner's reply was hesitant. Coupled with the word 'Lynton' it was sufficient to interest Nigel. The high-pitched voice of the Commissioner continued.

'Right, remind him to phone me from his office tomorrow morning.'

The Commissioner replaced the phone, looking thoughtful as he remarked, 'So, it seems all is in order down there at Notley, except for a local flu epidemic which has laid Markham, our Super, low. So you don't have to go down there and catch that, even if you don't catch anything else.'

Each could not help but join in as he chuckled at his own folly.

Quickly recovering his composure he continued speaking in a more serious vein. 'You will remember the reports you have just read. No need to remind you of the secrecy in this investigation. Being MI5 boys, you know more about that than I do.

'You will collect your expenses from here so I will now leave you. My secretary will be with you in a moment to let you have some funds, after which you can leave, and good luck.'

He rose abruptly and departed as quickly as he had entered.

Back at their chambers in Temple Gardens they tried to decide if any English people were connected with the West German security van robberies. They had no definite clues. The best that could be managed was the fact that two visitors to Lynton Hall and the son, Clarence, were in West Germany at the same time as the twelve million marks robbery took place.

'Our next port of call, it seems,' said Nigel, 'will be Hamburg.'

'You're not going by boat, surely?'

'Skip the funny stuff, unless you're trying for the job as Police Commissioner.'

'God forbid,' replied John

'In that case, let's be serious. We will fly in tomorrow and see what we can find out about this Fraulein Henkel in the Bismarck Flats in the Rusterstrasse 22, Hamburg. I am anxious to know if either her or the other woman who travelled with her is the one who asked me to visit my dentist.'

'We will be travelling light, I take it?' enquired John.

'Exactly. I have made reservations at the Bingham Hotel on a day-to-day basis, so we can stay as long as our business requires it.'

The flight the next day was a good one, arriving early in the afternoon. They went directly to their hotel where Nigel thought it would be as well to stay inside until dusk, knowing they would be less conspicuous in the half-light, for John and Nigel had used Hamburg before while in the service as secret agents on behalf of the British government. Hamburg had been their stamping ground, so they were known to many of its underground agents, from whom they had procured information which had made them a few friends but left them with many enemies.

The hotel proved to be very comfortable as they settled down in the small lounge after the evening meal. The street lights were just being illuminated as John glanced out at the evening sunset which was gradually being replaced by the glow from the city lights. They both saw the figure of a short man peering through the window at them who seemed as surprised to see them looking straight at him as they were at seeing him, for both recognised him as a notorious crook who had worried them years before.

'Welcome to Hamburg,' said Nigel as the startled face quickly vanished from the window.

'Now, I wonder what all that was about?' said John. 'He was as much startled to see us as we him. Was he looking as if he had some other object in view? We shall probably never know. One thing I am certain of, and that is I don't wish to see that swine again.'

'Hear, hear!' was Nigel's rejoinder.

Although neither welcomed their present assignment, the old excitement of being in danger was beginning to reassert itself, only this time they were likely to find their present problems overshadowed by past events.

From their hotel to the Rusterstrasse was but a ten minute walk to the street leading to the dock area. The

Elbe being in full flood, the ships appeared as if floating level with tops of the warehouse rooves, yet other new apartment blocks were replacing many of the older buildings with which John and Nigel were familiar, and even they were very few, for mostly wrecks of houses were all that could be offered as a form of shelter to the citizens of that post-war devastated city. Now the streets were completed to house a new generation.

They soon found the Bismarck flats at the corner of a junction of four roads. Nigel was the first to spot the building, saying, 'This is it. Here our two should now be. I expect they find it a little cramped after having the freedom of Lynton Hall.'

They were just about to cross the road when John said, 'Keep walking, Nigel. Don't turn your head. Carry on to the corner then turn the corner without looking back.'

Nigel followed John's order, knowing it was not meant lightly.

'What is it?' he enquired after they had walked about thirty paces round the corner.

'There is somebody watching the flat,' said John.

'I thought I saw two or three men together. They must have gone but there is certainly one now across the street, between two blocks of apartments, and as we went by on the other side he stepped back into the alley, as if he did not wish us to see him. There he is now, Nigel. Can you see him?'

'I can, and will go and investigate.'

Nigel put a cigarette between his lips as they approached the watcher together. Speaking with the accent of a dockside labourer, Nigel's German did not help him as he asked for a light. He was not to get one, for at that moment he felt something hard pushed into his back, as did John.

'We have been waiting for you,' came the guttural words behind him. 'Don't try anything but keep walking.'

Both were jabbed into the dark recess of the opening between the buildings while the lone watcher of the flat remained at his post. Nigel could see the pistol which was pushed into John's back and recognised it as a recent vicious model which was used for firing an explosive bullet, always a killer. There was nothing to be done except to submit to being blindfolded and their hands tied behind their backs before being ignominiously bundled into a dark Mercedes, which had been standing further back with a driver already waiting at the wheel. Their two escorts followed them in as the car moved into the main thoroughfare where the lone watcher of the building also climbed in next to the driver; the car accelerated away out of the city.

After travelling for about half an hour the car entered a wooded area, by the sound of branches brushing the sides, and it was clear to Nigel and John that they were going along little-used roads by the continued changing of gears and the constant turnings and splashing of water.

The car splashed through a ford which had been swollen by the recent heavy rains. The guttural voice was now swearing at the car having to go slower towards the deepened centre. They again accelerated up a steep hill, swerved to the right, travelled a short distance very slowly and stopped.

'Out you get,' said the same gruff voice.

Their eyes were next uncovered and their gags removed as they stumbled, still having their hands tied.

'What now?' said Nigel, as he looked around, but only the outline of a large building could be seen.

'You'll find out. Keep going,' was the only reply as once more he felt that venomous pistol thrust into his back. John also was receiving the same treatment as they were pushed into a doorway where they stood until the driver came with a torch which illuminated a large hall with bare stone walls on which were antlers and other trophies of the chase. They realized they were standing in a baronial hall of a very old castle.

Nigel tried again. 'When are we going to find out what you want with us, and why bring us here?'

'That, my fine friend,' said the voice, not sarcastic but less gruff, 'you will discover in a very short while. But first we must put you two to bed.'

Some hurricane lights had now been ignited, but they still waited until two of their gaolers came up from a basement saying, 'You can switch on now.' Electric bulbs illuminated the hall, from which a stone staircase spiralled to the floors above. This they were compelled to climb until they were high up in the building. It was quite impossible to know how many floors they had passed on their climb, but their chances of escape seemed remote.

Opening a door, they were taken along a passage in which strong oak doors had been fitted. These were further reinforced with iron studs and bars so it soon became obvious to Nigel and John that they were passing cells from which no sounds could be heard, but their purpose they were to find out later. At the end of the passage a door stood open which they were invited to enter. The room was furnished with two iron beds with straw mattresses. A single chair was the only other article. The gruff-voiced one promptly sat on it, at the same time indicating to his prisoners to sit on their beds while his companion waited outside with his pistol at the ready.

'Now we are nice and cosy.' He was again adopting his sarcastic tone. 'I want to know just what you two are doing in Hamburg, and also what do you know about twelve million marks?'

'Nothing,' said Nigel and John together.

'OK. Frisk them.'

The guard entered to give them a very thorough overhaul, but the precautions taken gave them no opportunity to escape, their hands still being securely tied behind them. The search having revealed no weapons, they were allowed to sit, but not until their cigarettes and lighters along with their wrist watches were taken, and then their hands were freed.

'Now you are here you can write down everything you have done since you have been in Hamburg, which group you belong to, your name, occupation and your address in the UK, the lot, and especially what you know about those marks.'

'Is that all?' enquired Nigel.

'No, that is not all, because if your answers are not satisfactory, you will be encouraged more forcibly to give the information I shall insist on getting from you.'

John said, 'That's all very well, but I can't write in your language.'

'That's no problem. We shall leave you here in the safe keeping of our guard as we shall be returning after we have been to Hamburg to bring someone who can tell. You have plenty of time to think it over.'

The door slammed behind him and was securely bolted on the outside as Nigel rushed to the door, listening as the footsteps died away.

'That's it then, John. It looks as if we're in a bit of a mess, and by the structure of this building I should say it was an old fort, probably built by the Templars. There's no telling what it has been used for since but by the look of the bars at the window, and no glass, we are going to be hard put to it to keep warm.'

'Who do you think the person is that they are bringing back tonight?'

Nigel pondered this question for a moment before answering. 'All I can say is I hope it is not the person I suspect it might be.'

John was quite sure that Nigel always kept his cards close to his chest, so did not press him further. They continued talking together, while the bulb above illuminated the cell in which they were confined: the walls were built of solid stone blocks, which on close examination showed scratches of names and dates ranging from 1940 to 1943. The surprising thing about them was that in every instance the forename was a feminine one.

'So!' exclaimed Nigel, 'I suspect it has been used to house women prisoners.'

They sat for the most part silently considering their chances of escape until the grey light of the dawn allowed them to observe the district around the fort, which had certainly been erected in a most desolate area.

In the distance appeared an expanse of woodland stretching to a range of hills. Inside their cell it was now quite light although the bulb was not extinguished, there being no switch inside, the wires going between the stones near the ceiling. Footsteps could again be heard as their gaolers returned.

They unbolted the door, kicking it open while standing outside with their guns. The same villain who had threatened them before came in carrying two school exercise books and pencils which he placed on the chair. Nigel and John remained on their beds. Standing half into the cell they were covered effectively by one as the other started to speak.

'We want to know all about you. You have just twenty-four hours to sign your confessions, and let it be what we want.'

'Don't we get any food or drink?' John asked.

'You do not. And think yourselves lucky you weren't one of those.' It was the one with the gun pointing at him who spoke as he waved his other arm towards the wall. 'They did not get any food or water until they had received some educational chastisement. It was only then that they got anything.'

He finished with a leer. The one who had put the books on the chair now advised them that if they got writing then perhaps they might get something when they got back.

'You filthy swines,' said Nigel.

This brought no further reaction except a sardonic grimace. The other gaoler said, 'Perhaps when the Englishman comes.'

'Shut up!' exclaimed his companion, as the door was slammed.

Nigel put his head to the door and heard one say, 'You fool, now they know it's an Englisher who's coming. It doesn't matter what they write now, we shall have to finish them off when we return.'

Nigel drew back, avoiding John's eyes, until footsteps could be heard returning. The door was thrust open and the one with the grimace said, 'You,' pointing his gun at John, 'outside with you. We're not leaving you two together to cook up anything.'

With both of them training their guns on him John was ushered out and the door again bolted securely on Nigel.

'We're not leaving you two together to cook up anything.' These words kept going through his mind as he viewed with desperation his present position.

# 6

Nigel noticed that John had left his book and pencil behind him, so it was apparent they were no longer interested in their stories, but only in disposing of them when they came back. Nigel sat on the chair. He had not time to tell John of his fears before he was removed.

Now alone he must take a fresh look at his surroundings. Two mattresses, the chair and the exercise books and pencils, which he had no intention of using, four solid iron bars at the window and a solid oak door completed his immediate world.

He had been in tight corners before, but never such as this with a prize of millions of marks, which these crooks were anxious to get their hands on. Did they think he was connected with a rival gang who had already had this treasure? It became clear to him that this was the case and in gang disputes lives mattered little. The sound of a car starting up sent him quickly to see a dark Mercedes leaving with two passengers. It travelled some distance before turning left. This would be in the opposite direction to that which they took last night, therefore it must be returning to Hamburg to collect the Englishman.

He looked down the outside walls of the mediaeval fortress which had been used during the last war but now appeared to be neglected, but known to the gang, in this desolate countryside. He was not likely to receive any help from a chance passer-by. Fortunately the sun had penetrated the cell and he was warm and felt no hunger. He speculated he must be about forty feet from the ground. It was then that he saw immediately below him a flat roof of a new portion built on the ground floor, used no doubt for the administration offices when the prison was occupied. The roof was some thirty feet down and he was behind iron bars, yet if he was to remain alive he must get free, find John and be away before the return of his would-be murderers.

The flat roof was sealed with bitumen. If it could be set on fire and he could shout loud enough, it might bring his gaoler to him. He could hear his keeper walking about from time to time and even smelt his own special brand of tobacco going up in smoke. He called out several times for water but except for something which sounded like 'nein', no other response was forthcoming.

The sun was beginning to sink behind the distant hills. How much longer, he wondered, before the others returned? He sat looking at the exercise books which he had brushed on to the floor. Then it came to him in a flash – a trick which he once saw demonstrated back in his old schooldays when he was a boarder at Marlborough. He looked up at the single bulb which had been alight all day. The mattresses could be pushed between the bars at the window. Without further hesitation, while it was still daylight, he would try the trick the boys did who liked to have a clandestine smoke in the dorms, when the possession of matches would have meant their being sent down.

Picking up the pencils he rubbed the ends against the stones to expose the leads. Then, pulling a thread from the corner of a mattress, he tied the pencils together. Next he pushed a mattress to the window, climbed on to the chair and removed the bulb, which he slipped into his pocket. The next part of the operation was going to be difficult single-handed. A few crumpled sheets of the exercise book in one hand, while the other held the pencils which he pushed into the lamp holder. Almost immediately they made contact with the points and the ends of the pencils started to glow as an arc was formed by the electric current. He held the pencils until his fingers felt as if on fire, when suddenly the paper burst into flames.

Dropping the pencils, and in the light provided by the flames, he was able to set fire to the corner of the mattress. It now commenced to smoke, giving off a stench, before the straw, which fortunately was dry, started to burn. Pushing the lighted end of the now flaming mattress between the bars, until most of it was hanging down like a torch, he let it drop to the flat roof far below where it landed with a thud, producing more smoke as the flames appeared to go out. Nigel's heart sank as he groped in the semi-darkness for the other mattress which he pulled to the window, tearing it as he did so; the straw interior he pushed out by the handful. He felt fear as he had never done before as he kept dropping bunches of straw into the rising smoke, until the mattress was nearly empty. Then he noticed a red glow appearing through the smoke on the flat roof. With renewed energy he wound the mattress around the little amount of straw still inside it to form a ball. This he pushed between the bars, allowing the empty mattress to hang inside the window.

The only illumination in the cell was the light from the roof below which was now well and truly on fire. He picked up the chair, moving back against the door, shouting, 'Fire, fire!'

He started to cough as the smoke was pouring in through the bars. The gaoler came stumbling along the passage a little quicker than usual, swearing as he did so. From the other side of the door he asked, 'What fire? No tricks or I'll give you fire!'

Nigel cried out, 'I can hardly breathe. I'm over by the window!'

The putrid fumes from the smouldering straw on the floor threatened to choke him.

'Quick, quick, I'm choking!' he called out once more, and he stepped to one side as he heard the bolts slide back, followed by the door being kicked open. The gaoler hesitated, to find the place in darkness, but seeing a head at the window which was all he could see against the glare outside, took a step into the cell and fired his gun at what he thought was his prisoner's head. At the same time he was struck by the chair which Nigel swung with all his power at that close-shaven, German skull. The gaoler crashed to the floor while his pistol bounced away in the darkness. Nigel now only had to swing around to close and bolt the door behind him, while the curses showed that his man was not out, and at this moment was groping for his lost pistol.

Nigel had to move fast to try and locate John, and in this he was lucky to find he was only four doors' away. John stood looking horrified, as he was expecting the gaoler to arrive to kill him. His look of utter relief as he gasped, 'My God, Nigel, I thought you had been shot,' brought a quick reply.

'Not yet, my hearty, but look sharp, we've no time to lose.'

Both raced to the stairs while curses and choking coughs meant the pistol had not been found. They reached the ground floor, running out into the courtyard to see the outbuilding well alight. John saw lights in the distance.

'Look, Nigel, those headlights.'

'You're right,' replied Nigel. 'They would be the others returning. I did not mention anything to you at the time, but I overheard them say they would shoot us when they got back. So we have got nothing to wait for. You may be sure they have seen the fire by now and will not waste time on that, but will start searching the grounds for us when they have discovered the one who thought he was putting a bullet through the back of my head. We'll go to the rear of the building, as I noticed the ground slopes downhill and with luck we shall find a stream of some sort; we are more mobile than they are as they cannot drive over rough ground, and I am certain none of them are in sufficiently good condition to run very far.'

Nigel and John made good progress, travelling about a mile until they came to the stream from which they slaked their thirst before continuing along the bank looking for firm ground on the other side. For as far as they could see in the light from the rising moon were marshes. Another two miles on they found there was firm ground the other side but the water was now swollen to a river, the depth it was not possible to tell, so that as much as they disliked remaining this side of the water it was necessary until they came to a ford. Another mile found them at a sharp bend in the river.

'This is where we must start looking as we go further downstream, for the current washes out the bank on a bend and deposits on the straight further down. So from now on look for any signs of animal marks going into the water.'

John, after about another quarter of a mile, was the first to spot the earth churned up by the water's edge.

The river was considerably wider here but the current had slackened. Nigel was able to confirm that this was the spot where many animals had entered the water. 'Here goes then.'

'Let's hope it's not too deep as to take us off our feet,' replied John.

So together, like two schoolboys, they entered the water which did not come above their knees.

'Good of you to hang on to me, Nigel. You know I can't swim.'

'These fords are often difficult to spot, John, and in a river this size there are often pot-holes up to eighteen feet in depth, so say no more about it.'

They climbed out on to a bank which was quite steep, but on reaching the top they found the ground levelled so that they could see in the distance a hut of some sort. On a closer approach they noted railway lines, and this was an unmanned signal box which had long been out of use since the introduction of automatic signals. A signal could be seen further down the line before a cutting between stone cliffs. It was near here that they found a large boulder which they dragged over a wire controlling the signal. They were able to alter it to stop. This accomplished, they returned to the signal box, the door of which they had no difficulty in forcing open, both dropping on to the wooden flooring where they lay exhausted and hungry, but for the moment feeling out of danger. It was very unlikely that they would be followed this far. John looked at his watch; it was now six-thirty. The moon had gone and it was still very dark with just the semblance of a false dawn in the east.

Both heard it at the same time, the unmistakable sound of an approaching train. John again looked at his watch, to the surprise of Nigel, who said, 'How did you come by that?'

'That's easy,' replied John, 'I had one on my other wrist

70

and managed to pop it in my mouth before they searched us. That's why I had nothing to say at the time. I only slipped it into my pocket after we were untied.'

'You mean to tell me you put it in your mouth before we left Hamburg?'

'I did, and it tasted foul. It's now five minutes past seven, and here comes the train.'

Fortunately it was travelling north, in the right direction for Hamburg. Soon the lighted windows of the carriages appeared. Then they heard the brakes being applied, the train slowing down as it passed the signal box, which gave them time to notice that the third carriage from the end was empty. They immediately climbed down from the box, following for a hundred yards to the back of the train which had now come to a standstill. Here they waited, watching the guard swing himself down and proceed forward along the track with his torch flashing along the wheels; he had gone a good distance past the empty carriage before they both made a spirited race to the third carriage. No sooner had they entered than Nigel opened the window, putting out his head to join the others along the train all calling out, 'Why the hold up?'

The guard returned, shouting out there was nothing to worry about, it was only a large stone fallen from the side and gone on the signal wire. Nothing to get alarmed about, we shall be off in a moment. The slamming of the windows as they were being closed was the only response he received in return.

The journey was resumed with two extra passengers, who began to recognise in the grey morning light the landmarks which they both knew so well from their wartime exploits in the district, which was but a few miles from Hamburg.

'We shall be coming up to a junction soon, John. Do you remember it's only five miles from the city?'

'I do,' replied John, 'and the train always used to stop there.'

As soon as the train arrived at the station, both walked back past the end of the train, jumped over a low gate at the end of the platform and into the street. John had another surprise for Nigel as he produced from the lining of his jacket a few mark notes which he always kept, as he put it, 'in a secret place for any eventuality.' They were thus able to enter the ticket office where Nigel bought his ticket, while John held back, obtaining cigarettes from a vending machine, one of which he offered to the ticket collector, who immediately placed it behind an ear. John, after he had received his ticket duly clipped, placed a cigarette unlit and followed Nigel at some distance to the refreshment bar.

John was a non-smoker, unlike Nigel, who said when they met up at the bar, 'My God, John, don't start on that. It will kill you.'

'That I have no intention of doing, but they may prove useful as a bribe.'

Having seated themselves at a corner table with fresh coffee, cheese and ham rolls, they enjoyed a meal which could not have been better relished than at any hotel in Hamburg. The cigarette, meanwhile, lay crushed in the ashtray.

They had ample time to finish their food before the train resumed its journey to Hamburg Central station, where they secured a taxi for the ride to the hotel. John 'accidentally' dropped the packet of cigarettes which was seized by a beggar before the taxi had moved twenty yards.

'A good turn?' enquired Nigel. John made no reply.

The state of their clothes and muddy shoes and trousers was unnoticed as they entered their hotel.

'A hot bath and bed, that's for us,' said Nigel. 'Having endangered our lives these last two days we have solved nothing and we still do not know who our enemies are. I can think of only one thing I can do, and that is to visit Fraulein Henkel, but this time I must go alone.'

The following morning, as they were both preparing to go down to their breakfast, there was a knock at the door which was opened by John to a diminutive page boy who had a large paper parcel. A signature was required and a gratuity accepted before John was able to see the label which showed it had come from Doyles Theatrical Dressmakers.

'That's for me,' Nigel called out. 'Last night, when you

were in the bath, I phoned the fancy dress hire people. It has to be returned later today.'

'You certainly are still as secretive as ever, but thanks for letting me tip the boy. I must remember to add it to the expense account with the cost of those fags which you refused.'

'Don't bicker, John. All's fair, needs must, and so on.'

So, chanting clichés at each other, they descended to the breakfast room in good spirits.

After an excellent meal they returned to their room, John to phone the airport to make reservations for their return to Heathrow, while Nigel, who had disappeared into the bedroom, returned some moments later dressed as a postman complete with his mail bag.

'Are you sure you don't want me to come along?'

'No thanks. I want you out of the picture for the present but I may want you later this evening, so make that flight back to be after midnight, just to be on the safe side. Bye.'

At that the door closed, leaving John wondering what he would be required for so late in the evening.

It was a very smart postman who went along the Rusterstrasse and approached the Bismarck apartments. To his surprise there were no signs of anybody watching the building, so he went straight into the main entrance, walked up to the second floor and sharply tapped the fancy knocker on the door of number five, which was immediately opened by what could only be described as a beauty. It was a young woman of considerable self-assurance and poise. She looked steadily at him as if melting the phoney costume from his back and replacing it with a shabby, ill-fitting coat. Her voice, when she spoke, was most regal, slightly condescending, yet at the same time giving him the respect which would have been his due as a postman. How he hated himself at that moment for his subterfuge as she enquired in the same silky tone which he had heard on the telephone back in London.

'Good morning, postman. Have you a letter perhaps for me?'

Nigel apologised, saying, 'I am afraid not, and I must admit I am not a postman but had to adopt this pose as I wish to speak to Fraulein Henkel.'

73

Matilda, who had just come from another room, on hearing her name mentioned, said, 'I am here. What does he want, Angela?'

'Angela's attitude had stiffened at hearing of the deception, while Matilda said, 'Your German does not deceive me, sir. You are English are you not?'

'You have found me out, Fraulein Henkel, but I must speak to you.'

'Certainly, young man. Come in and close the door. Now, before you say anything, I wish to know your name.'

'Sorry, it's Nigel Danton.'

'Very good,' said Matilda. 'Pray continue.'

Nigel half turned to Angela, saying, 'First of all I believe this young lady is British.'

'Correct,' answered Matilda.

'Well now,' Nigel gulped in embarrassment at the fixed stare from Angela. He floundered as he resumed. 'I and my associate John Royston are in Hamburg on the instructions of the British government to watch over the well-being of its nationals. People are not singled out; it is like the banks who send out letters to a certain number of their customers to ascertain if their accounts are correct. In other words it is a spot check to find if mistakes have occurred at the branches. There is nothing personal in this, you understand.'

'That is very commendable of your government, and where is your associate?'

Nigel blushed at having to invent a lie. Even Angela's lips curled slightly at each corner in partly concealed amusement at his discomfiture.

'He is at the moment engaged in paperwork at the Bingham Hotel, where we are both staying. But we have to return to London tonight, so that I'm pleased to find you at home.'

Matilda probed further. 'But why do you come to us dressed as a postman without any letters?'

'I had good reasons for doing so.' Nigel now felt himself on firmer ground, as he explained he was coming to see them two nights' ago but saw that the building was being watched from the other side of the road.

'That is right,' said Matilda. 'We noticed somebody so

74

we telephoned the police, who came and took him away, but who he was looking for we have no idea. But I don't like these prowlers, who are only too anxious to get in and steal.'

'In that case I am glad that no robbery was committed, and hopefully you will both be all right,' Nigel concluded.

Matilda seemed satisfied with this answer, saying, 'We shall be away from here for a few weeks, and going to friends in the country near Luneburg where Angela,' she turned her head slightly in her direction, indicating that this was as much of an introduction he could expect, 'can enjoy her horse riding on the estate. Her brother, who was here last night, has purchased two hunters at Frankfurt where he has now returned, but will be coming back to Luneburg where we shall again meet him.'

'Everything seems to have been taken care of, and I must apologise for deceiving you into believing me to be a postman, but in view of the watcher I felt it necessary to arrive inconspicuously. So now I can report back all is well. Would you both care to come to dinner at our hotel this evening when you could meet my colleague?'

'Thank you. Can I call you Nigel? It just happens we shall be leaving this evening and therefore must decline your invitation, but please extend our regards to your friend, John, isn't it? And thank you both for looking after our good and welfare. Now, what about a cup of English tea?'

'Thank you very much, that would be nice. I find this postman's uniform rather constricting.'

Nigel loosened the top two buttons of the jacket while Matilda left to prepare the tea. This gave Nigel the chance to speak to Angela to ask if it was she who telephoned him at his chambers asking if he had visited his dentist recently.

This time it was Angela's turn to be embarrassed as she searched for the reply which, however she answered, would involve Lady Dalsworth.

'Yes, I'm afraid it was.'

'And the reason, may I ask?'

'That, I am sorry to say, I cannot give as it involves another. But since we have now met I hope that disposes

75

of the matter, which I understand was of little importance.'

Nigel knew he was being fobbed off politely, but the
entry of Matilda with the tray of teacups allowed him no
further opportunity to pursue the subject, as the rest of
the conversation, to the relief of Angela, was taken up
with riding, horses, stables and brother Clarence, in that
order. Nigel took his leave, feeling he had still a long way
to go to establish any connection between the security van
robbery and the Dalsworth family – that is, if any
connection ever existed.

All had seemed perfectly innocent in the flat, except
their mere presence in Hamburg. The reference by his
kidnappers to an Englishman that same night that
Angela's brother, Clarence, was in the city seemed
extremely significant.

No notice was taken of him when he walked into the
hotel in his uniform, and John was momentarily taken
aback when he opened the door with his key. Having
explained all that occurred, Nigel said he was going to
invite them back for a dinner while John went and
examined the contents of their flat, but having seen them
he did not feel it correct. They were too ladylike. He said
to John, 'So I invited them to dinner just the same so that
we could have made a foursome, but they are leaving
tonight for a place I noticed the train ran through
yesterday on our way back to Hamburg. So, John, what of
the flight?'

'Yes, all arranged. Quarter to midnight.'

'Fine, our journey will be a short one and I fear we shall
have to visit our old friend Lady Dalsworth at Lynton Hall
after all.'

'If you could manage alone I should prefer it,' said
John, 'as I have had a phone call from my dear wife to say
they have had a burst waterpipe in the cellar at the Inn,
and the American tourists are arriving.'

'That's quite all right, John. Give Margaret my love.
Sorry to have kept you away but at the moment I think
you are right, one of us should be sufficient to go to
Lynton Hall. Two of us might look rather official. In any
case, we can do no more until other information comes in.

I hope it will not be another robbery. Now I must get rid of this postman's clobber and we'll go down to dinner.'

# 7

Nigel collected his car at Heathrow, taking John as far as Marble Arch underground car park, where he left him to get his Vauxhall to motor through the night to Margaret and the White Horse Inn in the heart of the Cotswolds. Nigel proceeded to his club in Piccadilly where he was to stay the night. As he entered, he was approached by the doorman who handed him a letter, the writing of which he instantly recognised as that of the Commissioner of Police at Scotland Yard. Inside the envelope was the curt notice, 'You are required to attend here at room 243 tomorrow at 11 a.m.'

He looked at the time. He had just nine hours to prepare his statement, but first of all he needed a good night's sleep, and that was a priority upon which nature would allow no precedence.

Nigel entered 243 to be met by the Home Secretary, who asked for his report which Nigel had only typed out two hours earlier. The Home Secretary waved Nigel to sit down while he took a seat at the desk. He took his time in reading Nigel's hurried account of his and John's exploits in Hamburg. Having finished, he sat for a while meditating, before he looked directly at Nigel, saying, 'It appears you nearly lost your lives, yet we are no nearer the solution. So I feel if there are no more incidents over there – although as you have written, there appears to have been an Englishman behind the scenes – we can leave the whole affair to the West Germans. I will not allow two of our most valuable investigators to risk their lives on a wild goose-chase.

'I have heard that the ones responsible for your

kidnapping have all been arrested, so you will have no fears from that quarter should you return later on. It appears a very alert German lady doing her public duty noticed a watcher on a corner near her home, who was promptly arrested. With a little inducement he betrayed his associates who were caught in a flat overlooking the Hamburg docks, along with a quantity of guns and hand-grenades. It seems the twelve million marks were stolen by another gang of crooks, and this lot thought you were one of them. So now you can return to your law courts work for a very long time I hope.'

'Thank you, sir,' replied Nigel, and was about to turn to the door when a sharp knock found them both facing the Commissioner whose face was full of foreboding.

He said simply, 'There has been another bullion robbery in West Germany which they insist is being masterminded by an Englishman.'

The Home Secretary's voice boomed out, 'Sit down, Commissioner. Then, turning to Nigel, he said, 'Well, it looks as if we shall have to keep you in harness a little longer. I don't like this at all. Why can't they solve their own problems? I feel they are using this Englishman angle to spare their men for other duties, but perhaps . . .' He paused to pick up Nigel's report before proceeding. 'Oh, I don't know, perhaps that was rather a foolish remark of mine.

'Well now, Danton. Are you ready to go along again?'

Nigel replied that he was and said he had intended visiting Lady Dalsworth.

'Just as you like,' replied the Home Secretary. 'I give you a free hand as before.'

Looking at his watch he said to the Commissioner, 'Give Mr Danton any help he requires and all enquiries to remain secret. Reports only to be made in this room.'

'Understood, sir,' was the response from the Commissioner as he rose quickly to his feet to open the door to the departing Home Secretary.

The Commissioner and Nigel sat looking through the reports for the next hour but could not arrive at a decision. They could formulate nothing from their contents to give them a single lead.

At last the Commissioner said, 'That's about it then, Nigel. I think your intended visit to Lady Dalsworth is about all you can do. I wish you luck, for I don't envy you.'

They both left together, Nigel returning to his chambers while the Commissioner went upstairs to, as he put it, some more headaches of home manufacture.

Lady Dalsworth was waiting at the front entrance when Nigel arrived five minutes later than his appointed time. She greeted him very pleasantly.

'How nice of you to come, Mr Danton. It's been a long time since we met.'

Nigel, acknowledging this greeting, thanked her for sparing him the time. He was impressed by her easy manner, showing no signs of nervousness at what he might wish to speak to her about. Yet she must be fully aware of what it might be. They went into the conservatory together where the maid, Rose, brought in tea as they sat facing each other across an ornamental white round table. Lady Dalsworth waited until they were alone, then she poured the tea, at the same time saying, 'So you have come to see me? I have been expecting you for a little while now, but I do not think I can help you very much. But please let me say this: I am willing and anxious to assist you.'

Nigel was sipping his tea and did not reply immediately; looking straight at her he said, 'Yes, I do admit I need some help.'

Again he lapsed into silence for he realized he was dealing with an extremely intelligent woman who had previously copied her husband's exploits in the dangerous world of confidence manipulation. She had been discovered by chance when she had lent a scarf to a policeman's wife and it had been recognised as one she herself had left near the scene of a crime.

Nigel now felt a direct approach would be the only way he could get the information he wanted as he said, 'As you may know, Lady Dalsworth, there have been several incidents reported in the press of robberies in West Germany which have several peculiarities similar to those which occurred in this country, of which I understand you have some knowledge.'

80

Lady Dalsworth was looking down at her lap. She looked up sharply at him but remained silent.

Nigel faltered at the direct stare but proceeded, 'It may be a coincidence that two of your household and one of your recent visitors are now in West Germany, staying near where the hold-up of a security van was made. I believe, and I am not alone in thinking this, that possibly a gang are using the presence of your two children and friend to conduct their affairs wherever they find they are staying, in order to cast suspicion in their direction.'

Lady Dalsworth, still looking directly at Nigel, said, 'Frankly, I think it is ridiculous to suggest they should be doing this, but I appreciate you telling me, though I feel you could have framed your statement better. But assuming what you say is correct, what do you wish me to say? Have you come here to question me?'

'Yes, I have a few questions to ask. Firstly, I should like you to know that I have found out that the voice which asked me to visit my dentist was that of your daughter, whom I have recently met, and to tell you that I am aware she telephoned me from here.'

'Quite right. Angela did so at my request. We wished you to know that we were aware of the happenings in West Germany which were not of our arrangement.

Nigel was dumbfounded at this clever piece of subterfuge, as Lady Dalsworth continued, 'We had Angela's tutor staying with us from India, who was about to return to her new home in Hamburg where she has retired, or I should say semi-retired. She had some dental trouble while staying with us so I recommended to her the dentist whom you had mentioned, and who has treated me since on several occasions. It was after I had told her that I realized she may speak about the German bullion robbery – she is rather talkative – so I felt we should let you know that we were in no way involved; I was quite aware that you would trace the message back to Lynton Hall and hoped you would judge us as being innocent of any connection.'

'You are quite right, Lady Dalsworth. I fear for your son and daughter, nevertheless. As I have said, they are being used in order to remove suspicion from the real culprits who may be impersonating them. Yes, I think I have a clear view of events now, which will mean returning to West Germany to keep a watch on both your son and daughter in order to trace the robbers.'

Lady Dalsworth glanced at her watch, saying, 'I heard on the news that there has been another big robbery over there, and it is all very worrying to me to think that my poor lambs might be in danger. I am glad you came to see me; you must come again when they return home.'

Nigel rose, saying, 'It will be a pleasure.'

'Now, Mr Danton, if that is all, I wonder if you could spare the time to take me into Notley? I am due to attend a meeting there. I had tried to arrange for the super-intendent's wife, Joan Markham, to deputise for me as she had done previously. But now they are both away on holiday.'

'Most certainly. I shall be happy to do so. But what about returning?'

'No worry about that, I shall telephone my personal maid, Olive, and she will come and fetch me. My chauffeur is busy with the gardeners, trying to tidy up the stables before Clarence returns bringing some more horses which he has purchased. They have a lot to do as he should be returning in ten days' time.'

Having deposited Lady Dalsworth at Notley, Nigel returned to London feeling that he had accomplished nothing by his interview. He arrived at his apartment to find a letter from John saying he hoped he would not be required for a while as they had roof trouble at the Inn, and he would have to be there until the work was completed. Margaret was well and they could cope with the problem.

'In the meantime I will make myself available when the worst is over, which should be within a fortnight. Take care, wishing you all the luck. God bless, John and Margaret.'

Nigel was just about to retire for the night when the telephone rang. It was from the Commissioner at Scotland Yard who said, 'We have had another robbery reported from Germany, and this time they are fairly sure it was an Englishman and woman who raided a small post office in a place near Hamburg. It was only a small amount of money which was taken but we are again expected to co-operate in view of the fact that they think our nationals are involved. Oh, by the way, I did not mention the name of the place. I'm looking it up now. Yes, it's called Luneburg. I expect you know of it as you were operating around those parts some years' ago.'

Nigel's immediate reaction to this latest piece of in-formation was of shock. Everything pointed to Clarence Dalsworth and his sister. But why should they wish to steal a few hundred marks? He said nothing to the Commis-sioner of his thoughts but promised to go to Luneburg the next morning.

Nigel arrived very early in Hamburg the next day, collected a car from the Embassy and was soon on his way to Luneburg, realizing how altered it was from his former days of hunting down the riff-raff of pro-Nazi sym-pathizers who were then still causing trouble in that district. He found the post office in a square in the centre of the town. Nearby, in the middle of a terrace of houses, was one which had a sign, Bed and Breakfast. Here he was able to have the use of a room for as long as he wished. The elderly widow who ran the establishment was not prepared to talk to a foreigner and knew nothing which went on outside.

Having deposited his personal effects in his room, he insisted on having a key which was eventually handed over to him before he left this depressive-looking establishment to walk out across the square in the warm, late summer sunlight to the post office. Here he found one of those shops which besides being a post office also provided the groceries and bric-a-brac for the locals. An elderly gent was behind the bars of a cage-like structure dealing with post material while two women and a small boy waited their turn for attention. Nigel employed himself in looking at some of the other commodities. He was spotted by a young lady who came in from a room at the back of the shop, asking him if she could be of any assistance. Nigel was about to say he was only waiting to be served with stamps, but decided this lie would probably be unnecessary as she could be one of the household.

'Is this the post office where the robbery occurred?' he enquired.

She recognized his English accent and responded, 'It is, sir, but what is your interest?'

Nigel's explanation was that he was co-operating with the police in the search for the robbers. She immediately became more friendly, saying, 'I am helping in the shop for the moment, assisting dad, as mother is upset and the doctor said she was to rest for a few days.'

She then went on to explain that the robbers had guns when they held up her parents and robbed them of 275 marks – all they had in the till. There was much more money contained in the safe but they seemed satisfied with what they had taken, and left without hurting her mother and father. The other customers had now been served and the father was busy with paperwork, still in his cage, as his daughter continued to explain further details of the occurrence.

The daughter, who was now speaking freely, Nigel estimated was about thirty years of age. She had dark hair and a very pale complexion, emphasised by her brown eyes which were magnified by the lenses of her spectacles. She explained she lived out of the town and had two children. Her husband having left her she was compelled to go out to work, which she found in a nearby shoe factory.

'It was yesterday morning,' she went on to say, 'when I was coming here for my lunch. Just after twelve it was. I was with two of the other girls from the factory when I noticed a man and woman come out of the shop and walk towards a car. I saw they were both wearing riding boots. I always look to see what shoes people wear. The tall man said in English, "Hurry, dear, or we shall be late for our meal." They both jumped in the car and drove away very fast.

'When I opened the door I saw something was wrong, as mother lay on the floor – she had fainted – while dad was standing over her and crying. The other girls had come into the shop with me and between us we put mother to bed, and while I helped to pacify dad the others went for a doctor. I have said all this to the police, who said my little knowledge of English would help to catch the robbers.'

The old gentleman had finished his paperwork but it was obvious he could not add anything to the story as he was still suffering from shock. Nigel thanked the young woman and hoped her mother would soon be well again. Also he turned to her father, saying he hoped soon the money would be recovered and thanked him for allowing him to speak to his daughter, to which he received no response as he left the shop. His next call must be to see Fraulein Henkel and Lady Dalsworth's daughter. It was obvious that this was the place to enquire where they would be staying, but he did not wish them to know what direction his further investigations might take.

Returning to his lodgings he enquired from his land-lady if there was any good hunting in the district, but she did not believe in that kind of cruel sport and never went out of the town, so she could not help him. A shoe shop with riding boots on display was his next opportunity. He entered to find nobody in the shop, but having given a hearty cough he was surprised to see a youth with flaming red hair shoot up from behind a counter, where it was obvious from the particles around his mouth that this was his lunch-time. He immediately apologised for not re-ceiving Nigel at the door, but explained the firm who owned the shop insisted that it remained open during the lunch-time.

'We are not very busy, so I always have a snack round about now.'

Nigel stopped him by suggesting he would like to be fitted with a pair of slippers. Nigel felt this would not add too much to his expense account; he could do with another pair, in any case. The salesman brightened up considerably at the possibility of making a sale.

'I see you have a very good show of riding boots in the window. Do you sell many?'

This seemed to have the desired effect as the response was immediate.

'Not many, sir, although my first customer yesterday was a lady who came in just as I opened and wanted a pair. I had great difficulty in fitting her owing to a bunion on her right foot, but I fitted her at last after I had given it a good stretch.'

He would have gone on had not Nigel steered him away by putting his next question. 'Is there much riding in the district?'

'Not a lot,' he exclaimed, screwing up one eye which he hoped gave him a thoughtful expression. 'The one big house near here where they have horses belongs to Baron von Ropner. It lays further south from here, between the main road and the river; I should say,' screwing up his other eye, 'about seven miles from here. That is the only one I can think of.'

His face relaxed from the effort of his concentration, so it was relief for Nigel to regain the street outside with all the information he wished to know. Tossing his slippers on to the back seat he turned the car south in the direction of the estate of Baron von Ropner.

The road south undulated in line with the river, the same river which Nigel felt sure was the one he and John had crossed some days previously. The road continued to twist and turn for about three miles before passing under a railway bridge, after which it veered away from the river where Nigel could see a lake which he was able to keep in sight until it was cut off sharply by a seven foot brick wall built alongside the road. Nigel felt this must be the commencement of the Baron's estate.

Two miles further along he came to the entrance; a typical entrance to a country estate, being arched in stonework fashioned with crests and emblems. Without hesitation Nigel turned the car into the drive through an avenue of elm trees of about half a mile to a building which was of the same red brick as the wall, and reminded him of the approach to Hampton Court.

It was after he had travelled about a quarter of the way along that he saw three people on horseback galloping across the park who would arrive at the house at the same time as himself. He slowed down and then saw they were riding to intercept him. Soon he recognized Angela by her fair hair which was streaming behind her as she urged her horse forward. The other was undoubtedly Fraulein Henkel, who was endeavouring to keep her horse on a level, while well back from these two was a man astride a hunter. The horse was big but the rider must have been tall by the way he sat in the saddle. Nigel could see all three were expert riders. The two ladies pulled up by the car, which Nigel had brought to a standstill. Fraulein Henkel was the first to speak.

'Hello, Nigel. We recognized your car. So you have come back again and you managed to find us here.'

'I have, Matilda.'

Nigel had heard her name mentioned by Lady Dalsworth so he felt he might just as well address her by her Christian name, especially as she had used his.

Matilda continued, 'We quite understand, and we shall all be very happy to speak to you as we have already been interviewed by the police.'

Clarence had drawn closer and was promptly introduced by Angela, saying, 'This is my brother. Let us all go into the house. Our host is away so we can talk without embarrassment.'

Thank you, that is kind of you. And as for my car, I must explain it is one I borrow from the Embassy and it so happens it's the same one.'

They all entered together and were soon seated in a very cosy room which, with its leaded lights in the windows, reminded Nigel of an English manor house. Matilda noticed him looking around and said, 'This is the Baron's English Tudor room.' She went on to explain the absence of the Baron, saying, 'The Baroness had foot trouble that required a slight operation, so they were going to spend a few days in Bremen where there is an excellent surgical foot hospital.'

They each sat quietly for a moment or two. It was Clarence who spoke at last. 'I have spoken to my mother by telephone, and was aware that you would be contacting me sooner or later. Both my sister and I have been interviewed by the police here as it seems we bear some resemblance to a couple who have been connected with robberies of quite large sums of money. They do not appear to be very sure of their facts, except a raid on a post office near here provided them with a description of a man and a woman which they say was very much like our own. However, the inspector said on this occasion they

87

were satisfied it was not us. This I took exception to, as I was not pleased with the officer's words "on this occasion". I told him I felt this was offensive, as his enquiries would prove that on *no* occasion would be his conclusion. At that I wished him an early success to his search, and perhaps he would be good enough when he succeeds to advise me. I must admit he was not too pleased when he departed.'

Nigel expressed his thanks for what they had told him, adding that he would be staying a few days in the district.

'In that case,' said Clarence, 'I hope you will come again. We are having a gymkhana here in three days' time and this annual event will be attended by many competitors and spectators. You must come along to that. We shall be having horse trials and we three will be joining in the events.'

Angela said, 'Yes, do come, please.'

Clarence again said, 'The Baron and Baroness will be back for that as the Baroness always presents the prizes. It will be an opportunity for you to meet them, having missed them today.'

Nigel agreed to come again, feeling more than ever that the recent robberies were nothing to do with Angela and Clarence.

Clarence suddenly jumped up. 'Before you go, you must see the two horses I have bought.'

Nigel rose at the same time as Angela, who insisted on coming to the stables with them. Later, as Nigel was leaving, he spoke of the lake he had passed on the road to the building. Clarence said it was on part of the estate and was well stocked with rainbow trout. At last Nigel was able to leave their very hospitable company, saying he would look forward to their next meeting.

The day before the gymkhana took place, Nigel decided to call in at the post office again at midday. And as he had hoped, the girl was there. She had arrived for her lunch and he wished to speak to her again. Also, he hoped her mother would again be in the shop. He was not to be disappointed, as all three were now there, and one customer who was just leaving as Nigel entered.

He expressed his pleasure at seeing them all together and a special smile for the mother who appeared to be fully recovered from her shock and was now busy checking goods at the back of the shop. With a voice which was anything but frail she enquired if Nigel wished to make a purchase.

'Why not?' said Nigel, picking up a bunch of salvias from a bucket by the door. 'I will have these, madam, which I wish to present to you.'

After she had received payment, she suddenly realized they were for herself. Her attitude changed to one of friendliness, which her husband was only too pleased to notice.

With very little encouragement all three tried to remember incidents which had occurred to them on that morning of their hold-up. The descriptions they gave were ample reason for the police to follow these up with their interviews with the two Dalsworths.

Nigel turned to the daughter who had not much to add to what her parents said. 'Did you notice anything about the car they used?'

But here again she was not too sure, only saying, 'It was something like the one you have. I did notice,' she added, 'the riding boots the lady was wearing were very tight, because she had a big joint on her right foot. I always notice boots and shoes, since we have to make them, and as she stepped into the car the foot on the ground showed up very clearly.'

'And that was all?' prompted Nigel.

'Yes, that's all,' she repeated.

Nigel wished them all good day as the husband came from behind his cage to shake Nigel's hand very affably before opening the door.

He was not clear what his next move should be. He had collected a wealth of information, yet his suspicions seemed to embrace more and more suspects. He must look further for the English-type man and woman if he was going to remove suspicion from Angela and Clarence who had had no need of money. But had they inherited the urge from their father which their mother had tried unsuccessfully to imitate?

He returned to his lodgings and advised his landlady that he would be away for a couple of days, but would be returning for the gymkhana. He would pay for his absence, as he wished for his same room on his return. She replied there would be a lot of visitors in the town on account of the fête at the Ropner park. So she could easily let his room. He found an extra ten marks was sufficient to pacify her need for extra cash.

He returned to the Bingham Hotel feeling amused at the thought of a landlady who knew nothing of what went on outside her house, yet she was fully aware when extra cash was possible. It was always Nigel's view that when he was in a fix with any investigations, to forget it all and spend his time thinking about amusing trivialities was a mental rest which often led to inspiration later. On reaching his room he put through a call to Scotland Yard, asking for news of any further developments at that end, only to be told by the Commissioner that he had no more to tell him, except that the super at Notley, Jack Markham, had returned from his vacation and would be keeping an eye on Lady Dalsworth.

'In fact, I said to him to follow her wherever she may go, even it it's Timbuctoo.'

Nigel replied he was keeping his charges under surveillance so that all the family would be unable to move without their knowledge.

Having completed his call he next visited the Hamburg police station but they had no further information other than what he had already gathered. Nigel returned to the Bingham, where he was to stay for the next two days, analysing all the items he had collected. He found clues were conflicting at every stage of his calculations. The likeness of the robbers at the post office to Angela and Clarence, yet on the other hand a woman with a large joint wearing boots. This could be the Baroness Ropner who also was to have treatment for her foot and was a keen horsewoman. Again, she and the Baron were not at their residence at the time. Then again, they would not be likely to rob a post office on their doorstep for a few hundred marks when they were probably worth millions.

The whole thing was contrary to reason. Were they behind the millions of marks robberies, and had they staged this little one in order to focus attention on to the

Dalsworths, knowing, as they would, about the hijacking of the security van in England? Knowledge of this, he thought, was a state secret, yet if they knew it was his place to find out, no matter what embarrassment this may cause. So his mind twisted and turned to find a starting point.

He must now see the Baron and Baroness, for at the moment he did not know who to eliminate. At least he was able to give a little confidence to Angela and Clarence, so the nearer he kept to them would be his best hope of finding who the perpetrators of these crimes were, for it was evident they wished to put the blame on them.

# 8

The day of the gymkhana arrived and this was made very evident by the brass band which had assembled outside his lodgings at Luneburg. Martial music was the accompaniment for his breakfast. When he had finished and looked out of the open window it was to see the bandsmen climbing into coaches to take them to Ropner Park. Nigel hoped they would play more dancing music when they arrived and less marching music.

Having waited half an hour to miss much of the traffic, he still found he had to join the procession as cars built up behind him, while at regular intervals along the way were signs indicating which way they should go, not that there was the slightest chance of going anywhere else as the side roads had all been sealed off by patrolmen.

It was a tedious journey. He could almost count the bricks on the wall as they proceeded at a snail's pace. This time he did not enter by the main entrance but was taken through a side gate along with all the other vehicles to be parked in rows on the turf.

The park had been roped off into various partitions for different kinds of sport. The fête proper had not started and the athletes were practising their skills. Nigel stood for a while watching those practising at the high jump and noticed some competitors came from the right while others from the left, and those from one side always put their right foot over first while others jumped with the left foot going over first. He moved further along to the weight-lifters exercising their biceps until he reached the stalls, where crowds had already gathered to buy articles which they could have probably purchased for less back in town, but as the salesman called out, it was for a good cause. Everybody was out to enjoy themselves, whatever the cause, which in any event was not made clear.

At the end of the row of stalls an iron fence separated the field from the gardens to the house. A gate through which Nigel entered led to perfectly kept lawns and flower beds. He was intrigued to see a line of holes a little smaller than one would find at the green on a golf course, but equally spaced across the grass to where he could see a group of people standing, one of whom was holding a crutch. He realized that it was this which had made the holes on the damp turf. They were so straight that as he walked alongside them he had the stupid thought that he had only to lift a corner of the lawn and it could be torn along these perforations. As he drew nearer the group he passed what could only have been the gardener looking down at his punctured lawn. Nigel felt inclined to suggest to him that it would be ideal to plant a row of potatoes, but felt it would be an unkind remark best kept to himself.

Somebody in the group was now waving their arm, and he was soon met by Clarence who walked a short way towards him, saying the Baron and his wife had just arrived and had been told that he would be expected. Nigel thanked him and said he was looking forward to meeting them. As they drew nearer, Nigel could see that the one with the crutch was undoubtedly the Baroness, who after the introduction said, 'I just had to look at my garden before anything else.'

Angela and Matilda turned towards him and smiled while the Baron, who had been speaking to another lady, turned to greet Nigel. He saw, to his surprise, that it was none other than Lady Dalsworth.

The Baron and the Baroness were both tall, having fair hair, although the Baron was slightly grey at the temples. Nigel thought he was about forty-five years of age and his wife perhaps a little younger. He was, without doubt, quite an imposing figure, and it was obvious they were both looking forward to today's events. Nigel having joined the group, they now all walked into the building together. The Baron and his wife retired to their apartments, leaving Lady Ursula, as the Baron put it, to mind the fort for the moment.

As they left she turned to Nigel, saying, 'Now, Mr Nigel, I suppose you are wondering what I am doing here. The fact is, after the children had left me and since your visit, I had a very uncanny feeling I was being watched. So when one of the gardeners had seen on two occasions prowlers in the park, who hastily tried to conceal themselves whenever he walked about doing his work, he thought he should tell me.

'I was going to phone the police, but thought I would sneak away,' she gave a little smile, 'to see my darlings. The Baroness Catherine had invited me a few weeks' ago, but it was not until I heard my children were here that I decided to come. I was here the other day when you came but had a slight migraine so could not leave my darkened room, and I understand naughty Clarence did not tell you. So now, what have you discovered to remove this cloud which seems to follow our family around?'

Nigel had to admit that he was still collecting information to be able to assure the West German authorities that their problem was in no way connected with our country. As Nigel spoke he looked down as if in thought, but really to observe Lady Dalsworth's right foot, which appeared quite normal.

The Baron now joined the group, saying Catherine was resting. 'I'm afraid the foot operation has taken it out of her a bit, poor dear.

'It will be the first time she has not seen the show all through, but she will be along to present the prizes later.'

He was dressed in his riding habit, and was joining the other contestants later in the afternoon, when Clarence and Angela would also be competing in some of the equestrian events, which left Nigel as the sole male escort to Lady Dalsworth and Matilda to see some of the other trials of strength in the tug of war and swinging the hammer. Later they watched the men's and boys' races which always preceded the horse trials.

Although the afternoon was warm and sunny it was not sufficiently dry for the ground to be good for the horses, which the Baron had previously said would be rather heavy going. Angela and Clarence did well in the obstacle course in which the Baron did not take part. He had saved his hunter for the three mile hurdle race in which Angela and Clarence wished to try out the horses. There were sixteen riders. All got off to a good start and the positions kept changing as they moved out into the country. Clarence was well ahead at the half way mark, but from then on his horse started to weaken and he was quickly overtaken by others in the field. The Baron was well back but was moving up, coming level with Angela near the woods. It was as he was passing her that his horse shied and he took a tumble, but was quickly back in the saddle, when he and his horse seemed to regain even more speed and, passing all the others, came home amongst resounding cheers for his gameness and good horsemanship. He completed the course in record time, against West Germany's best well-known jockeys.

Baroness Catherine arrived on the course in a vintage Rolls Royce, which was kept especially for this occasion when she would present the prizes.

It was while the last winners were collecting their trophies that Nigel glanced at Lady Dalsworth, whose face had turned ashen; he stepped forward in time to prevent her falling to the ground, and with the help of Matilda seated her near one of the booths. He had noticed her continually looking around and he knew it was not at the exhibits but more as one who is looking for another person. In her case it was a hunted, frightened look. She soon recovered after an attendant from the ambulance tent had provided her with a stimulant, and it was fortunate that they were able to join the Baroness in the Rolls Royce for the return home.

Nigel decided he must have one more talk with Lady Dalsworth before he left. She told him it was the heat and the excitement of the afternoon which had caused her to feel faint; there was no other reason, for she was quite well. But still Nigel noticed the look of being hunted had not left her.

As the evening approached many of the cars started to leave before the fireworks started, which was often the sign of a general stampede before darkness closed in. Nigel remained watching the rockets and set pieces from the terrace, accompanied by his host who showed no signs from his fall. Others of the party who were guests joined them with several of the household staff.

Nigel finally left, unable to get any more information from Lady Dalsworth. He thanked the Baron and Baroness and regretted he could not stay for dinner as he had reports to make out back in Luneburg, where he was expecting a telephone call from London. He felt this was the best excuse he could make in view of the fact he had not brought his dinner jacket with him. The Baron accepted this reason, saying he must come again. Nigel thanked him for the enjoyment of the afternoon and said that would please him very much.

Nigel left to find his was the only car standing in the centre of the grass enclosure, where a solitary attendant stood with a torch to guide him off the premises. As he drove away he was still perplexed at the number of clues he was collecting – yet they appeared to lead nowhere. He was truly baffled. However, the day had been a welcome change for him so that he felt completely relaxed as he retired to his room. He was making out no report that night and felt no twinges of conscience at his mild deception of the Baron as he climbed into his bed and sweet oblivion.

The next morning, while at breakfast, the landlady told him a gentleman wished to see him. He was waiting for him in his car outside. Would he go out to him when he had finished his breakfast, but not to hurry, he was quite content to wait. When Nigel stepped outside he was surprised to see the Baron seated in the back of a Mercedes; on being invited to join him the Baron said that the chauffeur had been sent on some errands so he could speak to him alone.

The Baron said, 'Do you remember when I fell off my horse?'

'I do,' admitted Nigel. 'I was watching several together when you took your tumble.'

'Exactly,' exclaimed the Baron. 'Now I wish you to know that it was no accident.'

The Baron felt in his waistcoat pocket and produced a revolver bullet. This he handed to Nigel, saying, 'This was the cause of my fall. It was discovered in the rump of my horse when I returned to the stables. Fortunately my groom did not notice it, only the wound which I said must have been caused when we went through the thicket. So we are the only two who know. I have said nothing to alarm the ladies who are all returning to Lynton Hall along with Clarence and his two horses. They will be leaving later this afternoon. My wife hopes to go later on when the treatment to her foot has been completed. In fact, I too am looking forward to accompanying her at the same time.

'In order to put you completely in the picture I must go back to yesterday when I fell from my horse. I had been sparing the animal until I reached the woods when both the Dalsworths were more or less riding together, although I could see that Clarence was still slightly ahead. It was then, as we approached the gamekeeper's hut, that I decided now was the time to urge my horse for the final race home. As I passed Angela my horse jerked me out of the saddle. We were passing the hut – that I am sure about now I have had time to think about it – when I thought I heard a shot, but with the noise of the hooves and the fact that shooting often occurs in the woods, it did not register as being of any significance at the time.

'Now, on thinking back, I am wondering if the shot was meant for either of the Dalsworths. I had passed on the outside of Angela so that it would have hit either her or her horse on the right side, but as it happened I am glad nothing happened on such a day, and equally happy that they are returning today.'

Nigel wondered if the Baron was more concerned with the spoiling of the gymkhana than any injuries likely to be suffered by others. After a moment's thought, for the Baron had now finished speaking, Nigel said, 'I think I would like to examine the spot where you took your toss. I suppose you have not reported this to the police?'

'No, I have not done so. I felt you would be better at investigating this mystery, which I am sure was not intended to be a fatal shot or it would have been aimed higher. No, I do not want any publicity, which would certainly happen if the police were brought into the affair.

By all means, come along. Shall we say ten o'clock tomorrow? I will be waiting for you. You do ride, don't you?'

'I do,' admitted Nigel.

'In that case, come round to the stables. I have a hunter; it's quiet and a good beast to handle. Ah, here comes my chauffeur now. Until tomorrow, then.'

Nigel went back into the house more perplexed than before. One thing he was pleased about was that the English group had returned to Lynton Hall where it would be easier for him to be, back home, so that not only would he be able to watch over his own affairs but would also be in closer contact with the secret branch of the CID at Scotland Yard.

True to his word, the Baron was waiting when Nigel arrived promptly at ten o'clock. He had alread saddled up two horses and the one Nigel was offered was indeed a splendid-natured animal to handle, an experience which he had not enjoyed for many a long day. In cantering across the park Nigel realized the exhilarating pleasure he had been missing, and was starting to think of the possibility of owning one of these obliging animals when they arrived at the gamekeeper's hut, where the Baron started to dismount.

Leaving their horses at a little distance they approached cautiously, looking at the ground for signs of footmarks. The ground was still damp and the grass crushed into many impressions. The inside of the hut had two small windows. One was on the side while the other looked out to the race-course.

Nigel said, 'To shoot at an object as fast as a racehorse requires perfect timing to score a hit at what I should say was only twenty metres away. I also consider two people were here, one looking out of the side window to note the speed while the other would fire as soon as the horse's head came into view. The bullet would then impact about half-way back along the animal in line with the rider's right leg.

'Now, I take it this is the point where you accelerated passed Angela?'

'You are quite correct,' said the Baron.

'In that case, one watcher at the side window would call out "now", and the one with the revolver would fire immediately the horse's head came into view, but you were travelling much faster so the bullet struck further back, missing your leg but hitting your horse in the buttock.'

Nigel looked out of the front window and noticed a recent scratch in the wooden sill which would be most likely caused by a firearm resting on it in order to steady the aim. Next he bent down to where there was the distinct impression of a boot-print. When he placed his own shoe in the same place he found that it was about one third of an inch longer, and as he took size ten, this would mean the one who stood there had a size eleven foot.

Next he went to the side window and here again was the distinct impression of a boot-print, but a much smaller one, and by the imprint of the heel he judged it to be that of a woman. He spent a lot of time looking at several of these impressions while the Baron remained outside so as not to confuse Nigel, who had noted that the right shoe at the side window had left a print showing it was wider than the other, or that it was on a foot with an enlarged joint.

Coming out of the hut Nigel said, 'From what I can gather there were two people in here – a man and a woman. The man would have been over six feet while the woman would be about five feet six or seven.'

He made no mention of the marks caused by the woman's right shoe.

'And that is about all I can judge. Having a woman as an accomplice is a good excuse for them being here should they have been discovered.'

'Quite, quite,' agreed the Baron. 'Well, no point in worrying further. I'm glad they are no longer in danger here.'

'I agree,' said Nigel, 'and I do not think they will try anything of a similar nature back in England.'

Mounting their horses they slowly walked them back. Nigel spoke of an old fort or castle some miles to the south.

'Yes,' said the Baron, 'there is a very old fort; something to do with the Knights Templars. It was patched up during the war and used as a prison, mostly occupied by women who were employed on the land thereabouts growing vegetables, so I understand. But the soil in that locality is so poor it will hardly grow weeds, let alone anything else. I believe they were badly treated at the time, but since then the place has remained derelict, and it's such wild country nobody ever goes there. Although, now you have mentioned it, there was some kind of blaze some days' ago. No fire engine would bother to go out there, so unless there was a danger of starting a forest fire it would be left to burn itself out, and I expect that is what happened. But it certainly lit the sky, being night-time.'

They had now reached the house, where Nigel was invited by the Baroness to stay for lunch. It was then that she enquired if they had enjoyed their ride, to which Nigel was the first to admit it was a great pleasure as he had not done so recently.

'I saw you go as far as the hut together. Is it used now?' she enquired of her husband.

'No, dear, it is not. I am going to have it pulled down.'

'That pleases me. It so spoils the view of the woodland, and if it is not used now. Horace the footman told me that one of the maids saw a light over there the other evening. It appeared to be coming from the hut. He went over to it the next morning but found nothing. All the same, it could conceal undesirable people, so that when it is removed I shall be able to enjoy my view of the trees without seeing that nasty little pimple.'

She smiled at her own joke. Then, changing the subject, said, 'We are alone at the moment, but hope to join up with our friends again shortly in England, which will give some of our staff a chance to take their holidays. Some will remain, as we are having workmen in and they like to be supplied with drinks.'

'It's all been arranged, dear,' said the Baron.

Nigel soon after took his leave, saying, 'Perhaps we shall meet again in England.'

Going back to his lodgings in Luneburg he collected his belongings and took his leave of the landlady, who said she would always have a place for him should he care to return. Nigel hoped this would not be necessary, but kept his thoughts to himself.

Arriving back at his hotel in Hamburg, he gave himself the luxury of a hot bath before telephoning John to meet him in the Piccadilly club the following day. John promised to do so for he knew Nigel would not wish to consult him unless he was in a fix. So he said he was anxious to know all that had been going on; things were now normal at the Inn, and Margaret would be pleased to know he was needed by his old companion.

Nigel next telephoned the Commissioner at Scotland Yard to arrange a meeting in room 243, where all the information gathered could be gone over again and again to try and find some connection between the family at Lynton Hall and the robberies in West Germany.

But first he must speak to John, for he had an uncanny knack of solving a problem which would escape the perception of an expert. John was one of those very rare people who could not concentrate on a single subject for very long yet had a considerable amount of common sense and had luck in his diagnosis of a complicated problem, such as the present one. Yes, Nigel certainly wished to talk to him.

Nigel caught an early flight back to Heathrow the next morning, going straight to his club, where he found John already waiting to hear of his latest adventures. After they had found a corner seat in the lounge and refreshed themselves with a whisky sour, Nigel unburdened himself with the facts and figures, to which John listened intently but made no attempt to interrupt or stop the flow of words.

At long last, when he had heard all the facts, John said, 'I must think on this one. Perhaps another?' looking at the empty glasses.

These having been recharged, John proceeded, 'I think you will continue to gather clues, but at the same time will be placing yourself in danger. I personally think the only way we can solve this problem is to stage a play ourselves and let the mystery ones dance to our tune for a change. That is the only way we can find the culprit or culprits to this series of robberies. This is the only way, for I fear these people know of your connection with the investigation and are one step ahead of any preparations you are likely to make. Also, now they are not only threatening with pistols but are prepared to use them. We shall have to arrange that only a few know of what we intend to do. But leave that for the moment, we can judge better after tomorrow when we have heard if the Commissioner has discovered anything fresh while you have been abroad.'

'You're right, John. I have been too close to everything and cannot see the wood for –'

'That's it then,' said John, cutting him short. 'So now what about a game of snooker? It'll take your mind off work for a while.'

And so the evening passed. John eventually retired at the club while Nigel went back to his rooms in Temple Gardens, where he fell asleep as soon as his head touched the pillow. John sat upright in bed sifting through all the information which, as he had told Nigel, was a mass of clues which took one into a blind alley. There was nothing to connect them with each other. He decided that to sleep on the evidence was the best medicine, and he too was soon fast asleep.

They both arrived the following morning at room 243 at Scotland Yard within minutes of each other to find the Home Secretary was present and deep in conversation with the Commissioner. They continued talking for another ten minutes while Nigel, having been invited to look at the papers containing the points to be discussed, seated himself at the desk at the far end of the room, where John joined him to re-read their own reports with the observations added alongside by the secret intelligence staff. Also there was the home news and more from the superintendent at Notley, which showed that he had kept close observation on the comings and goings at Lynton Hall.

At last the Home Secretary, having finished speaking to the Commissioner, crossed the room to thank them both for their perseverance, and said, 'I'm afraid very little has come to light so far, but unless we get any more urgent calls from West Germany, I think we can still concentrate our attention on looking for any connection to their troubles in this country. I for one will be very happy if you find no evidence; but I must be certain of this. That is why

I wish you both to give this your utmost attention until you are satisfied with the results you obtain.'

Turning to the Commissioner he said, 'You will explain what we have been discussing, and stress the reason for very tight security to be adopted.'

The Home Secretary departed as the Commissioner came and sat down by them, saying, 'Now we have to formulate a plan which I hope will disclose the rogues in this nasty business.'

# 9

Lady Dalsworth was sitting again in her favourite chair near the conservatory, looking across the park. It was a fine June morning as the mist rose from the lake to reveal the sun, promising another warm day. She felt extremely contented now that Clarence and Angela were again safely back in her keeping, as she was wont to imagine. She could hear Matilda in the music room, while her children had gone riding together, as they would often do in the mornings. Clarence was very keen to keep his new acquisition of livestock in good fettle for a point-to-point meeting held in July at a nearby estate.

She could see them approaching now, at a steady pace. They were a very affectionate brother and sister. Clarence had never had an interest in the opposite sex at all, yet it was evident that they were extremely happy in the common interest which they had in horses. Angela came into the room through the conservatory open window, while Clarence took the horses to the stables. When he joined them later it was to hear that they were discussing a musical evening.

'We have not had one for some time now,' Lady Dalsworth was saying.

'Actually, six weeks,' said Clarence.

'The time is immaterial,' rejoined his mother. 'Anyway, it's sufficiently long to be without some music.'

'Quite right,' agreed Angela. 'I think it's a splendid idea.'

'That's fine. I will send out the invitations for a week today.'

Lady Dalsworth was quick to add, 'You need not attend,

you can always go and knock the little snooker balls about, can't you?'

'Yes, mother,' Clarence agreed. 'It's just a matter of taste, I suppose. But I may put in an appearance later on, if that would be all right?'

'Oh, yes, that would be a splendid idea. Then you can assist Olive and Rose with the refreshments. It looks so homely for the son of the establishment to be seen doing a little domestic duty. Angela cannot as she will be the pianist.'

Lady Dalsworth said this with a smile, which Angela was pleased to imitate, while Clarence looked bewildered. But he also could not resist smiling as he said, 'Oh well, yes, I suppose so. Yes, all right.'

Angela, in a little friendly dig, said, 'Thank you, sir.'

At that he hastily departed before he could be saddled with other domestic duties even less to his liking. Nevertheless, he had no option but to comply with this one, under the direct gaze of his mother and the look of amusement from his sister.

The musical evening at Lynton Hall had been arranged for the middle of June. Lady Dalsworth, Angela and Matilda had each helped to select the guests; amongst them were the local superintendent and his wife, the vicar of Notley, Mr and Mrs Gayford of the nearby Dolls House, also Nigel Danton and his friend, John Royston. Nigel was most enthusiastic in accepting the invitation, telling John he was always very keen to hear a pianist playing entirely alone – a fact that surprised him as he knew Nigel was distinctly unmusical. But he remained silent in view of this zeal to attend.

The Baron and Baroness von Ropner were expected to come, using their light plane, and were to have stayed the night, but storms over northern France caused them to cancel the visit.

Twenty-four people were assembled in the music room when Angela took her seat at the piano on the rostrum. She commenced to play some of Chopin's Nocturnes. The E flat major was well played and appreciated. Some of the Preludes followed until the room was bathed in a sense of peace which affected all the listeners.

The stirring sound of the *Revolutionary Study* in C minor was the sign for the interval, when the two maids, assisted by Clarence, passed amongst the guests distributing cups of tea or coffee and light refreshments. Angela had played perfectly, not a note out of place. She showed her pleasure by the slight blush of appreciation at the well-merited response.

Clarence was doing his best and enjoyed the looks of thanks he received from some of the villagers, who appreciated being waited on by one who they considered far above their station. Clarence was doing famously until, handing a cup of coffee to the superintendent's wife, he spilt some of it, fortunately only on himself; he had presented the cup to her right hand whereas she took it with her left, which caused the cup to rock backwards and forwards in its saucer. John, who was sitting on her left side, was not quick enough to avoid a few splashes coming his way. Nigel, sitting near John, gave no indication that he had seen this incident, he being still under the spell of the night's music, for his eyes were constantly watching Angela, who had left the rostrum and was speaking to her friend, Matilda.

After the interval, Angela resumed with lighter music, including Bach's haunting *Melodie Sicilien* in G minor, finishing the concert with a lively little tune, *Les Sylphides* by Cussons.

And so another musical evening at Lynton Hall came to a close. John and Nigel, motoring back to London through the night, hardly spoke a word until John broke the silence by saying, 'What did you think of tonight's little play? Was it a charade to show us how cosy they all are at home, or did it have deeper motives?'

Nigel was intent on his driving. After a considerable time he replied, 'Yes, you are right, it could be either.'

The next morning both reported to room 243 Scotland Yard, where the Commissioner was waiting to speak to them. He had still more arrangements to make to ascertain if the robberies were being controlled from this country. Interpol were busy on the continent. But any investigations here he wished to be kept as private as possible.

106

'Now, as you are aware, Jack Markham, the super at Notley, has been keeping a close watch on events down there, although during his recent holiday – at Bournemouth I think they stayed – Lady Dalsworth escaped his attention by going abroad; but as you were on hand, Nigel, you were able to see all that occurred on that occasion. Now I would like you to meet Jack Markham.'

'We have already met,' said Nigel. 'He was present at a musical evening to which we were invited at Lynton Hall last evening. Both he and his wife were introduced to us.'

'That's all the better, then. I'm glad Jack is keeping in close touch. He will be retiring very shortly and I would like you both to check all that has been happening. He will then give you the details of all that has been going on. I have already briefed him by phone so you need only make arrangements to meet him and he will know what it is all about.

'Once you have this then I think we can leave things as we have done in the past, unless we get any more scares from West Germany, but as they have arrested one gang and no doubt put any others into shock for the time being, I think you can leave things until you hear from me. Or, of course, unless you have spoken to Markham and you think you can pin somebody down in this country, which I hope to God you can't.'

The Commissioner looked at his watch. 'Blast the time,' he uttered in the same quiet voice, 'I have only ten minutes to get to Downing Street.'

John and Nigel walked out into the warm air in the street. No breeze stirred the atmosphere; the heat was oppressive, which foretold stormy weather. They went along to their club where the air conditioning was a pleasant relief. It was here that Nigel put through a call to Jack Markham at Notley, only to be told that the super was at court but would be in his office tomorrow morning. He had been expecting them to call and would stay until they arrived. They had little to do but wait until the morning, so they stayed in the club, going up to the billiard room later where they started a game. Suddenly all the lights failed, accompanied by a crack of thunder which was the beginning of a night of noise and torrential rain. The constant flash of the lightning illuminated the room every few seconds.

John remarked, 'We have saved a bit of money not going to the disco tonight. We've got one laid on by the Gods.'

'And when did you ever go to a disco?'   'Heavenly disco. Quite a thought. It makes me more anxious to try the other place.'

By the morning all the storm had gone, along with the heavy atmosphere, so that they were able to leave London in bright sunshine which was drying up the steaming roads, making driving once more a pleasure as they entered Kent and on to Sussex, reaching Notley police station at ten o'clock. Jack Markham was there to meet them with the usual drinks accorded to special visitors. Nigel opened the conversation by speaking of the musical evening they had attended two nights before.

'Sorry I was not able to see you yesterday,' said the superintendent (stopping Nigel's views about music). 'We have some flooding around here and I was out until a very late hour. But now the water has subsided and fortunately nobody had water in their buildings. I understand the storm passed on to London later. I hope you found the roads all right?'

'Yes, fine, thank you. No trouble at all. It looked as if there was some water lying in Lynton Park as we came by.'

'That's good,' responded the superintendent. 'I know the son, Clarence, had been waiting for water to fill up his lake. So now he should be more than satisfied. However, should it spill over into the road then we shall be concerned. I have kept a watchful eye on the comings and goings there, as you no doubt are aware, but I have very little to tell you, and I hope I never have to put in a bad report. As you know, I am often invited there and I am friendly with all the family, so that the duty assigned to me has not, as you may guess, been all to my liking.'

For the next few moments there was silence in the room, which was interrupted by a knock at the door. It was the desk sergeant to report that he had received a telephone message that there had been an accident at Lynton Hall. A workman had fallen from the roof of the building and was seriously hurt. An ambulance was already on the way.

'It should be there by now, sir.'

'Right,' answered the superintendent. 'tell Sergeant Davis to take Birke with him and get along to the Hall straight away. Take statements from anybody there, whether they are eye witnesses or not. Also find out if anybody was up on the roof with him. Names and addresses, the lot. I want to know did he fall or was he pushed? Come back and make out your report. Oh, and send Birke on to the hospital to get the doctor's report. Should the man still be alive, Birke is to stay with him and take down anything he might say. Also to phone me in two hours' time. That's about it. Get them going.'

'Sir,' the desk sergeant replied, and promptly closed the door behind him.

'Not pleasant. Not pleasant at all,' repeated the superintendent. 'Well, gentlemen, I have a lot of paperwork to do, so if there is nothing else I'm afraid we shall have to finish our conversation, but I have made out a report in this envelope that you can take back. Also I will send you a copy of the sergeant's report and the hospital statement in a couple of days' time.'

Nigel and John expressed their sympathy, which they hoped the superintendent would convey to Lady Dalsworth.

'Certainly I will. I shall be going up there later, as soon as I have got sergeant Davis back and heard what he has to tell us. And see if I can glean anything else which may throw light on the incident.'

John drove on the return journey passing Lynton Park. The Hall was bathed in sunlight, giving it an atmosphere of peace and tranquility, the flooded foreground showing an inverted picture from the placid surface of the water. He continued driving until they reached Green Park in London, where he handed over to Nigel, who went on to his chambers. John telephoned Margaret and then walked to a store near Trafalgar Square to choose some electric light fittings which were required in the new cocktail lounge they were constructing at the White Horse Inn.

Nigel, meanwhile, found his secretary, George, up to his

eyes in official forms and documents, all marked for immediate attention. Nigel joined in the work of helping to sort out the urgent ones from the more urgent ones; so for the rest of the day it was business as usual.

☆ ☆ ☆

The following morning, amongst the first batch of letters was one from Lady Dalsworth in which she explained the accident at her home, writing that the man who had fallen from the roof was an old associate of her husband who was in the army in India at the same time, when both were taken ill in the mountains.

'Clarence had met him in the village and decided to give him a trial at work on the building. He was good at what he was given to do, so my son arranged that he should stay. In fact, the work was proving to be of a permanent nature as the stonework kept crumbling away.

'At the time of the accident the man – Thomas Atkins – had just mounted a ladder to adjust some slates which had moved during the storm of the previous day, and while doing so a lightning conductor staple came away; it appeared that he must have held on to it while adjusting the ladder which was close alongside, and as it came away from the wall he lost his balance and fell, striking the balcony which bounced him on to the flower bed. This must have saved his life, poor man; he is now in the cottage hospital and is concussed and has a broken arm.

'The superintendant, Jack Markham, came to see me and was very sympathetic. He told me you had both been with him for a short while that day. I expect it was about those robberies in Germany. I hope they catch all the thieves.

'Oh, yes, I had nearly forgotten to mention that at the same time as Thomas fell from the roof, Clarence and Angela were out riding when her horse stumbled in a field where the moles had been active. She was thrown from her horse and struck her head, rendering her unconscious. Clarence brought her back and she was put straight to bed where she remained, hardly breathing. The doctor examined her and said it was a nasty knock she had received but, I am glad to say, he said she would be quite all right in a few days' time.'

This news disturbed Nigel more than he could have thought possible. He was beginning to think of Angela more and more each day, and was determined to find some pretext to visit Lady Dalsworth as soon as he felt his true interest would not become apparent by going too early.

John, meanwhile, had finished his shopping and phoned Nigel from his club in Piccadilly to say he would call to see him for the latest information from Notley, and then return to the country where he would be needed at the White Horse more than ever during July and August. When John arrived at Nigel's chambers he found the promised letter from Markham had arrived, which confirmed much of the information supplied by Lady Dalsworth, which Nigel had insisted he should read first. The report from the hospital explained that Thomas Atkins had been admitted with a broken forearm and was concussed. He was still unconscious. No other injuries could be diagnosed, although there was no reaction on the right side of the body. A specialist thought it might be a paralysis brought on by an electric shock, but would not express a firm opinion at that stage. The patient was healthy and the heart action normal.

John, having read the reports, found Nigel was more concerned with Angela than the man who had fallen from the roof. The police were satisfied that it was a pure accident so had no more to add. Nigel insisted that he should pay another visit to Lynton Hall, yet John could see no reason for him to do so and was not going to be drawn into supplying an excuse for him to go again. He said he would be returning home, as nothing else had happened either here or in West Germany to warrant him staying in London on the scant information they were able to collect.

John was aware that he might be needed again if or when the Commissioner at Scotland Yard decided on the action they had discussed in room 243, and was prepared to play his part. Nigel seemed a little crestfallen at his unwillingness to assist, but agreed there was not much they could do, and George was rather inundated. So he would attend to his own business a bit more once again. John now realized that Nigel was going to concentrate on his career and mask his feelings or the thoughts he had for Angela's own problems.

So John returned home, while Nigel busied himself with his work. Angela recovered quickly from her fall and was out riding every day with Clarence, who was excited by the news that they had both been invited to the gymkhana being staged at Belvoir Castle. Thomas Atkins was still unconscious in the hospital.

Nigel after a few days found the pressure of work had lessened to the extent that George could manage fairly comfortably, which would afford him the excuse to visit Notley again to enquire at the hospital how the patient was progressing. He could then follow this up with a visit to Lady Dalsworth to give her the latest information. Yes, he decided he would do that. It would not be unseemly of him and he might meet Angela to compliment her on her recovery. Something on those lines would be in order and not too presumptuous. So once again George was left to do the paperwork which could be completed before the summer recess, and he too would be able to enjoy a spell away from the city.

# 10

Nigel stood at the bedside of Thomas Atkins. He had made a good recovery. The arm had set and he had full use of his hand. Unfortunately, his right side was competely paralysed and he had lost his power of speech.

Nigel stood for ten minutes while the old gentleman tried to interest him by making gestures with his left arm, although it conveyed no meaning. Nigel continued to nod at a face showing intense effort by mouthing and screwing up his eyes in an effort to impart knowledge.

The nurse came forward as Nigel waved goodbye, to seek the doctor who had been attending him. The principal was seated at a desk just off the main corridor, next to the reception desk, and it was obvious he was waiting for Nigel on his way to the exit. He explained that the case was a very conflicting one. He could only say that in his opinion the patient had received an electric shock. It would appear (so he admitted on the evidence of the electrolysis department) to have been caused by a charge of static electricity stored in the lightning conductor which had been broken below, and on a dry wall the current would be contained in the cable.

'Now, to get back to my line of duty,' the doctor continued, 'that is to try electricity to induce the nerves and muscles to respond. Once we get a response, then the chances are that the power of speech will return. We have had the patient out of bed and assisted him in walking, and only this morning there was a slight movement in a leg muscle, which is encouraging, but it's early days yet. It will be an exciting experience for us if we get him back to walking and speaking again.'

Nigel thanked the doctor for sparing the time to give him such an explicit version of the case.

As Nigel took his departure he noted the name on the desk was Mr J. Brooks and the qualifications showed that he was the head surgeon – and he had been addressing him as a doctor.

Slowly driving away he could not make up his mind whether to call at Lynton Hall. He drove even slower as he neared the gates but proceeded past, the avenue of elms almost enticing him to enter, but he resisted the urge; no, he would leave it for another day. As he increased speed he kept reciting to himself, 'Faint heart never won fair lady.'

Another day passed seeing him helping George once again, but he could not give work his full attention. He kept telling himself he was a fool not to have visited Lynton Hall when he had the chance, for then he had a perfect excuse, but now he had not. The following day only a few letters needed attention and he was wondering how he could occupy his time when the telephone rang. It was picked up by George, who promptly handed it to Nigel, saying, 'It's for you.'

Nigel accepted the phone and was greeted with the dulcet tones which had so intrigued him many days before when it had asked him about his dentist. It could be none other than Angela Dalsworth sounding so ethereal on the telephone. No-one else had a voice which had such charm, such friendliness. It was a voice which could infatuate any man. He swallowed hard before replying to the question, 'Is that you, Mr Nigel Danton?'

'Yes, it is. How nice to hear your voice.'

'Thank you. Lady Ursula wanted to know if you would care to attend a musical concert; it is only me. It will be next Tuesday at eight o'clock. And bring your friend along.'

Nigel replied that he would be delighted, but he could not bring his friend with him as he had returned to his own home in the Cotswolds.

'Oh.' Her voice sounded a trifle disappointed.

Nigel waited awhile before calling, 'Hallo,' but there was no reply. The receiver had not been replaced, so he waited patiently, wondering if she would speak again. George had been watching the look of frustration, almost anguish, on Nigel's face; his own face registered a sympathetic smile.

Suddenly Nigel jerked to attention as the soft voice, almost cajoling, said, 'Lady Ursula said if you are coming alone, it would be better for you to stay the night. She does not like you to motor back so late at night when you can do so very easily the next day. Would that suit you?'

Was the voice anxiously inviting or not? He couldn't tell, nor did he care as he promptly answered, 'Thank Lady Dalsworth for that very kind thought. I shall be delighted.'

'Until next Tuesday, then. Goodbye.'

The 'good' was on a high-pitched note, sinking away to a low, almost breathless 'bye'.

The telephone was replaced very gently, while after a moment Nigel did the same, continuing to look at letters he had already seen, while George, who had been half-listening, was now bending even lower over his correspondence than seemed necessary.

The rest of the week was taken up with plenty of calculating and tidying up, for it was the end of their financial quarter and the holiday season was now upon them. Nigel was anxious that all papers were put safely under lock and key, for the lady cleaners would clear everything, no matter what, so that when one resumed after the break it was difficult to recognise one's own compartments. Nigel was always extremely careful after a previous catastrophe when the title deeds he was dealing with were left out on such an occasion and finished up in the incinerator.

Saturday came. George had left for his summer holiday, while Nigel looked around the office but could not settle to do anything. He telephoned a few friends, then phoned John who invited him down for the weekend. This Nigel accepted as John said he would like to be updated about the visit to the hospital.

The following morning Nigel was on the road very early. It was an extremely pleasant ride on a hot day, the movement of the car providing a welcome breeze with the essence of the countryside which always seemed to commence as he descended Broadway Hill and entered the Cotswold country. He arrived at the White Horse Inn at noon. Both John and Margaret were outside and gave him a true welcome with the home-brewed ale which was a speciality of the house.

After Sunday lunch, John took Nigel for a ride around the district through off-the-track roads, while Margaret sat quietly in the back seat of the trusty old Vauxhall. Nigel, sitting next to John, was able to give him the lastest information on the robberies. But for all the concentration and all the clues the problem remained unresolved. Margaret meanwhile, occasionally glancing out of the windows, was busy with her crochet.

John was beginning to realize that Nigel was forming ideas of getting closer acquainted with Angela, but he was not sure that he wished to be consulted on such a delicate subject. He would not give Nigel any satisfaction as regards his chances of attracting Angela.

The evening was spent playing their favourite game of cribbage, and no more was said about Nigel's desires that night. So after a mini-weekend he departed the next morning, his problem still unresolved.

# 11

On his return to London he no longer noticed the countryside. He was wondering who had invited him to the musical evening. Was it Lady Dalsworth or Angela? He would have preferred to have thought it was the latter, but her indrawn breath as she said, 'Oh,' on hearing that John would not be coming did not encourage him. John, though, was a happily married man, so why should he think as he was doing?

Arriving back in town he felt undecided what he would do to pass the day and found some interest in visiting the zoo, but still found little solace in watching the animals, some of which had their mates with them. His feelings were now growing into an obsession, like a youth having his first mental love affair with a distant Hollywood actress. And yet he was a bachelor, a confirmed bachelor, who thought he was immune to the so-called attractions of the opposite sex.

He returned to his chambers and retired, soon to awaken in the early morning feeling as a schoolboy feels on examination morning. He found himself singing in the bath, something he had not done for a very long time. Having dressed he took a hasty breakfast, although he had all day to spare for a two-hour journey.

No sooner had he entered his car than he was arriving at Lynton Hall. He remembered nothing of the driving. It was as if he had travelled on a magic carpet, so easy and effortless had everything appeared.

Clarence was on horseback near the gates. Giving Nigel a welcoming wave he galloped off across the park towards the stables. He felt a surge of jealousy within him that

Clarence was able to ride with Angela whenever he wished. Yet to feel as he did about brother and sister was absurd. He must pull himself together and remember he was on a special assignment for Her Majesty's Government, in which the Home Secretary had given him explicit instructions which were to be communicated to nobody else.

Yes, he must remember he was of some importance, but he must not disparage himself if he should be falling in love. It was a natural feeling which afflicted the most highly respected and important men in the realm, and they were no less because of it. Leaving his car on the gravelled section, he walked towards the front entrance to be met by Angela coming out.

She thanked him for coming, saying, 'You could not induce John to accompany you, then?'

Nigel again felt jealous that another should be considered while he was there before her, wishing to claim all her interest and attention.

'No,' he replied, 'John expressed his regrets as he was very busy at the Inn. I went down to see him and his wife on Sunday and he was sorry to have to refuse, but hoped to be given the opportunity another time.'

Nigel searched her face as he said this, hoping to find a trace of vexation or annoyance on those serene features, but nothing ruffled them; he could not gain any information from the Madonna mask she was pleased to wear. Then suddenly the mask slipped as, switching on a bewitching smile, she said, 'Do come in. I know Lady Ursula is in the drawing room with Matilda, and they will be pleased to see you.'

Nigel entered the room to find them seated opposite each other at a small table playing chess. Lady Dalsworth rose immediately and walked towards them.

'We are glad you have decided to come, and you can stay the night, can't you?'

Nigel assured her he could do so.

'We often play chess together. It's supposed to be a man's game but Matilda and I enjoy it. Do you play, Nigel?'

Yes, he admitted, he did play.

'In that case you will find Clarence a keen player, and I know he would like a game.'

Angela now asked to be excused. 'I did not go riding this morning, so Clarence had a gallop without me. I find as I am playing tonight it would be better if I have a little practice, so if you will pardon me, I shall be in the music room.'

Nigel enquired about the man who had fallen from the roof, only to be told that there was little change, but just a small amount of muscle movement could be noticed.

'The physiotherapist and doctors are using all kinds of electrical equipment on him and they think they will obtain ninety per cent mobility, as they term it. So we do hope he recovers. He has been such a help to Clarence on the roof repairs. Why don't you go along and meet Clarence? He should be back at the stables by now, or if he has left he should be in the conservatory.'

Clarence was in the conservatory, calling out to Nigel as he approached, 'Sorry not to have given you the official welcome just now, but my horse, Twilight, was late for his medicine. The vet insisted he should have it regularly for a slight cough and I was ten minutes late getting him back. Anyway, now you are here. That's the main thing. We shall have much the same amount of people as last time, but now the Baron and Baroness Ropner will be coming. They fly into Bournemouth, where we have sent Charles to pick them up. They should arrive back here about four o'clock.

'Come in and have a drink. I keep some in the billiard room next to this.' He waved his hand at the foliage. 'This is mother's pride and joy. So I am often handy when needed. Anyway, here we are.' He opened a door behind a large shrub of deep red bougainvillaea and they entered the billiard room.

'Do you play?' he asked.

Nigel assured him he did.

'Right then, what would you like? Snooker?'

They both played very skilfully but Nigel proved the better, and Clarence insisted on another game in which he was beaten by an even bigger margin. Clarence expressed his pleasure at being able to play with such an experienced

119

player. There was no time for further play as the Baron and his wife had arrived and gone straight to their apartment.

Clarence now showed Nigel where he would be staying for the night. 'They have arranged some sort of tea party in the afternoon room at four-thirty, where we are all expected to meet for tiffin. So I hope you find everything you need.'

'Yes, thanks,' replied Nigel. 'I will just go back and get my things from the car.'

'Oh, by the way,' Clarence interjected, 'we shall not have an interval in tonight's programme. I do not think I accomplished my task to mother's liking last time. So we shall finish early and a formal dinner will be held for the house guests only. That is why mother asked you to stay the night. You having met the Baron, she felt it would be nice for you to meet again.'

Nigel thanked him, thinking to himself how thoughtful of her to remember things such as this. That is what comes of good breeding, he considered. But at heart he was still an investigator, and a change of opinion was always possible.

When Nigel entered the afternoon room he found that the small houseparty who would be at the dinner that night had already assembled. The Baron, spotting him first, came forward, saying, 'So, we meet again,' shaking him firmly by the hand. The Baroness was looking extremely pleased as they took their seats at the tables from which they overlooked the gardens. Olive and Rose, the two servants who Nigel had previously seen, served the teas without this time having any assistance from Clarence – his mother no doubt thinking after his slight mishap with the coffee he would be no more successful with the strawberries and cream.

Afterwards they all walked on to the terrace to observe the arrival of the rest of the guests for the evening.

Angela played light-heartedly the well-known pieces from operas such as *The Gipsy Princess*, Puccini's *Manon Lescaut* and Borodin's *Prince Igor*. Sailing through the repertoire her fingers hardly seemed to touch the keys. For an encore she played with even greater expression

Ducas' *The Sorcerer's Apprentice*, to the delight of her audience who now departed, except for the local vicar, Mr and Mrs Gayford from the nearby Doll's House and the superintendent and his wife, who had been invited to stay to dinner.

Clarence had decorated the dining-room with trophies from the chase, which he had on loan from a taxidermist. These he had hung on the walls to give the effect of a baronial hall as a complimentary gesture to Baron Ropner, who he knew was a keen huntsman. Lady Dalsworth was not very enamoured at the idea of stag and boar heads looking down at them, their glass eyes shining in the flickering lights from the candelabra as if balefully contemplating their own bodies being consumed before them. But she forebore to complain to Clarence of this little foible of his. The vicar took Angela's arm as they went in, next followed by the Baron and Baroness, Nigel and Matilda, the superintendent and his wife, Joan, Mr and Mrs Gayford and Clarence escorting his mother, who took her seat at the head of the table.

Olive and Rose, with the aid of a footman, saw that the dishes arrived in a smooth and silent manner, while the footman later dispensed the wines. In fact, it was a traditional, well-ordered dinner party.

The Baron was particularly pleased with the arrangements, which he knew had been made for him. Nigel was seated next to Matilda, while Angela sat next to Lady Dalsworlth and facing Clarence. The conversation flowed smoothly as the meal progressed, and assisted by the wine, stories began to be told. The superintendent told of his early experiences in the police force when he was on duty in the docks of London. Nigel gave an account (no longer a state secret) of something which he had experienced while with MI5 with his associate John Royston. After this the vicar, who had said grace at the commencement of the meal, added a few stories in a lighter vein.

Nigel found Matilda a good companion and very knowledgable as she continued to acquaint him with various items about bird life in India. While she was speaking to him he noticed she would often look around the table with a puzzled expression, and each time her glance came to rest on Joan, the superintendent's wife. Nigel, in turn, would look towards Angela, but she appeared to be more interested in talking across the table to Clarence, although she occasionally turned to the vicar to make a comment in reply to his sustained efforts to create a conversation. At one point Nigel did look up to find Angela looking hard at him, her large, deep blue eyes staring in a way which showed no recognition. For a moment or two he was nonplussed, then it dawned on him that he was not being looked at but being looked through. Angela was deep in thought and Nigel felt deflated at the prospect of only being an object which she could not even see. The moment passed as Lady Dalsworth called them to attention by proposing a toast to Thomas Atkins who was still very ill.

'We wish him well.' Glasses were charged as each one repeated the toast.

Matilda, who had not spoken to Nigel for the last few minutes, having appeared deep in thought while still looking across the table at Joan, said sufficiently loudly for all to hear, 'I would like to tell a story, if I may. It is one which I would often give to my classes in India and was more for the benefit of those who were left-handed. Angela has heard it, although I know she is right-handed.'

Angela gave a slight smile and nod while still looking at Nigel, then appeared to notice him for the first time. Nigel's returned smile was met with a little pursing of the lips as she turned her head towards the vicar.

Matilda continued, 'It is not a short story, so I hope you will not be bored.'

The reaction suggested that all were anxious to hear what Matilda had to say. Joan, however, looked a little uncomfortable as Matilda started to speak.

☆ ☆ ☆

'Now, this is about a very old man who lived in a country cottage not far from Frankfurt, and I want you all to try and imagine it is the old man telling the tale; I must apologise if my voice does not sound like his.'

Smiles greeted this little quip, as she spoke in a quiet yet audible voice.

'It was a cold but dry day in February when my three children and five grandchildren visited me. I have lived here alone for several years. It so happened that I had just put some fresh pine logs on the fire when they entered. The grandchildren pulled up their stools to the fire, ready for their cocoa, which was due to arrive when their parents had made tea for themselves. This suited me very well as it meant I would not have to move from my seat by the fire to prepare a drink. Now this story is for my grandchildren who were all under ten years of age and it is usual for me to tell them a story on these occasions when my children come to give me a tidy-up. It was not long before they said, more or less in unison, "A story please, grandpa."

'To this I was hard put to think of anything until, like a flash, I remembered a story my father used to tell when I was a lad. It was one which went back to his own schooldays. But I must digress for a moment. "Where are you going, grandad?" they all called out together.

'"I will not be a moment." I went to the toolshed at the back and, sure enough, I found what I was seeking, and then returned to them at the fireside.

'Now, to get the right feeling I will repeat it word for word, as far as I can remember, as he told it to me many, many years ago. So as I speak I want you to think it is your great grandad who is telling the story.

'When I was ten years' old, or thereabouts, I lived with my father and mother in a little house a long way from here. It stood on top of a hill. Now, from my bedroom I could see across the valley to my school, which stood just before another hill. A river flowed through the valley in front of the school. It was a view I never tired of looking at, except for the school. About forty boys went there; the girls went to another in the village.

Now, the boys' school was run by a master named Mr Abbott, while his wife ruled over the class I attended. Her name was Mary, not a blessed one, either. The lads called her Old Mary. She was very strict and believed in giving educational chastisemet, as I heard her say to a temporary teacher. This educational correction consisted in slapping the top of the head with hands which could have done duty for a goalkeeper. The boys who were left-handed were compelled to write with their right hand. I was left-handed, as the eldest boy in our family has always been. I felt myself her star pupil for this correction, as after every treatment I was able to feel the bumps on my head which had been caused by her rings.

'Now, one day at school we were told to write a story of our own invention. I could think of nothing else but my educational chastisement, and the knowledge bumps which had developed by this process. When the exercise books were collected for her to examine I watched her face change from pink to ashen white. It was then that she slapped my book down and called out my name. I then had to go out to the front of the class, where she was already rolling up her sleeves in order to give me another helping of correction. I did not have long to wait as the blows started raining down on my head, accompanied by the words,

> "Your composition is stupid
> Your phrases are disgraceful
> Your spelling is atrocious
> and
> You have got to learn how to write a story."

'I was then confined in a cupboard in total darkness which was reserved for brushes and brooms, and not released until late after school, which I knew was so because I could see the other boys climbing the hill about a mile away.

'When I arrived home my mother did not say anything, although I was late; but my meal was on the table, which I soon ate. Then, collecting my comic papers, I went upstairs to read them in bed. That evening it came over dark very quickly and the clouds started to rush by just as they are doing now.

'I must have fallen asleep, for when I woke up it was still dark, although the moon had come out. Clouds were rushing past it faster than ever. Then, as I looked at them, a light from the school caught my eye and seemed to get

124

bigger as I watched it. It wasn't a fire because it was not that kind of light. It grew bigger and bigger until I could see nothing but this bright light.

'I dressed quickly and went out of the house to try to get near it. Then, suddenly there was a terrible noise as the light split up the centre and started to roll up from the middle, like a curtain parting, to reveal a country I had never seen before. My school was no longer there; what I was looking at was entirely different.

'The countryside was covered with all sorts of trees; there were oaks, beech, orange and lemon, pine, poplars and palm trees with grape vines clustering around them, and in the distance were cactus and coconut trees. It was a wonderful sight. I stepped between the oak doors and down a flight of steps before reaching a road which curved away into the far distance, but not to my school, for in its place was a most astonishing building made up of all kinds of architecture. There was a large, castle-like entrance half way up the side of the hill, also turrets and a keep, and also a pagoda, a Chinese temple, a mosque next to an American skyscraper, Russian onion roof domes, minarets, spires and, oh, all kinds of buildings – all in one.

'I was drawn to this building, which stood where my school should have been. My feet seemed to take twenty foot strides as I went towards it, and as I drew nearer I found the road led to a small entrance at the side of a thatched cottage which was still a part of this huge structure. I knocked on the door, which was opened by a very old man who bid me enter. As I passed by him I noticed that his white beard came down to his waist. He smiled very kindly at me. I walked to the centre of the small room and then turned round to find he had completely disappeared. Standing in his place was a young girl of about my own age; she had very fair hair and bright blue eyes which seemed to grow bigger as she said, "Follow me."

'Going to the far end of the room she opened another door from which a flight of steps led down to a cellar where there were many barrels and bottles of wine. Some had been used as there were empty bottles and many corks laying on the stone floor. There was a table and stool near an arched wall. A solitary candle stood on the table and a bottle which had only been half emptied. Again she spoke, saying, "I will leave you here. Do not drink anything – it is all poisonous."

'I sat for a long time feeling thirsty. The candle continued to burn brightly, but did not get any lower. As it reflected in the bottle my thirst grew in intensity. It was then that I noticed some mice on the floor, running around and drinking the drips coming from the bottles. They appeared to have come to little harm. In fact, they were becoming more lively. My thirst grew so that I was tempted to drink from the bottle. Although I was never allowed to drink wine my thirst was so great that I reached out for the bottle. At this moment I heard footsteps on the stairs. I looked up and saw the most handsome boy I had ever seen, and I knew we could be friends.

'Speaking in a soft voice he asked if I had drunk anything, to which I replied I had not drunk a single drop. This answer pleased him; he smiled then went towards the brick wall on my left where he moved a wooden stick fixed between the brickwork. The bricks opened to reveal a golden cage which had golden gates studded with diamonds and rubies. He opened the gates and told me to step inside, saying, "I will not be coming with you." He gazed at me. Never will I forget that look of longing as he did so. I also perhaps gave him the same impression as I continued to look in his direction long after he had disappeared from sight. As the lift rose the sound of bells was so musical that I wished it would continue. The higher I went, the louder the sound. It was becoming lighter so that soon I would be able to see what was in the rooms above.

'Then suddenly I was wide awake in my bed. My mother had just entered the room to say there had been a terrible storm in the night. My window had blown open and my clothes had fallen from the chair. She started to pick them up as she said, "I have just had a message from one of the teachers at your school to say it will not be open today because of the floods, but you are asked to write a story and you can go tomorrow."

'Mother suddenly stopped, then said, "The rain must

126

have come in through the window. Your trousers are soaked. They smell as if you have spilt wine all over them. What is this?" She had picked up a cork which I recognised as a wine cork with a big top like I've seen sometimes.

'"Where did you get this from?" she enquired. Then, not waiting for an answer, said, "Oh, I know what boys are. You pick up anything to stuff in your pockets. Now hurry and get up. No school does not mean you can lay in bed all day long. You have some homework to do."

'I had finished my homework and the next day I went to school. There had been no flood but I had a new teacher. On the night of the storm the schoolhouse had been struck by lightning and although the master had not been hurt, Mary had. The lightning had struck her left arm, the one which had the hand with the biggest rings on it, which had done so much to knock sense into me. Yes, I had a new teacher and Mary never came back to the school again.

'That is my story and here is the champagne cork to prove it. My father gave me the cork which had the inscription YGTLTWAS on the top. It came to me that this was the beginning of each word, "You've got to learn to write a story."

'That's it. That is the story your great grandfather told me many, many years' ago.

'"What about the cork?" enquired Karl.

'"Oh, yes, bless my soul, I nearly forgot it."

'I searched through my pockets, finding it inside my jacket. I held it up as if it were a jewel before handing it to eager hands to pass around, their eyes looking at me with awe and at the figures on the cork top.

'I was glad nobody had gone to my shed at the back. I would have to sweep up the pieces of cork in the morning. Stretching out my left arm I reached for my pipe. It was then that I remembered the youngest had been missing for a while as I was telling the tale, he being too young to understand many of the words. I thought he may have spent his time with his mother, but he did give me a strange look as he kissed me goodbye. I wondered, yes, I would go and have a look in the shed. He may have been

127

in there. Directly I opened the shed door I saw the imprint of a baby's shoe inside.

'But then he would have been too young, although I'm still wondering at that cheeky smile of his as he went out holding his mother's arm and waving his left hand at me.'

☆ ☆ ☆

Matilda had finished the story, rising from the table waving her left arm. And as if by a pre-arranged signal, the ladies all rose at the same time to withdraw, while the Baron stood and clapped to be joined by the other men who continued clapping until the footman had closed the doors through which the ladies had left.

When the men were alone the Baron said, 'You know, our country abounds with this kind of story, and though it is supposed to be for children, there are a lot of hidden meanings for adults.'

Nigel said, 'Yes, I became aware of that when I was on special duty in your country just after the war, and I felt at that time it would have been an interesting subject to have studied. We also have some of those stories here, the principal one which everybody knows being Lewis Carroll's *Alice's Adventures in Wonderland.*'

'Exactly, and I believe Matilda is a very astute person to think up that story for her girls, although I wonder why she told it to us tonight?'

Nigel was thinking the same, but before he could reply the ladies returned and all the party went into the conservatory, where coffee was served. Later, when they were seated, Lady Dalsworth asked Jack Markham when he would be retiring from the force.

'In about a month's time,' he replied. 'Joan and I hope to find a place in Bournemouth and once we are settled we shall not be too far away, and as Joan's sister lives there she will have company. In any case, we shall look forward to seeing you at any time.'

'But not all at once, I take it,' said the vicar amid laughter.

The superintendent said they would like to be excused now as Joan had a slight headache. 'We have both enjoyed the evening. It will be a memorable one amongst pleasant company.'

Very soon afterwards the Gayfords left, taking the vicar back to Notley with them. After a short interval the remaining retired to their rooms. Nigel returned to his bedroom thinking of the night's story. What had the Baron meant? Was he implying that Matilda knew something unknown to the others and was trying to convey it in a story? Why would she do this? Why not openly tell them, unless she herself was implicated in a conspiracy. What had the left hand, which she had continually spoken about, meant? Why did she look so hard at Joan, who was left-handed, even before she commenced her story?

Nigel looked across the lawn from his window. The moon was sufficiently bright that he switched off the light by the dressing table. At the same time some of the other bedroom lights, which had been reflected on the lake, were now being extinguished. He sat at the open window. It was a warm night and he felt no need for sleep. He only wished John had been there this evening. He was very quick at finding an answer to an enigma. He was just about to try and get some sleep and was in the act of turning round when he saw a flash of light on the lawn, which he realized could have been caused by somebody opening a downstairs door. He opened the window and stepped on to the small balcony, from where he was able to see the whole length of that side of the building.

He saw the figure of a woman wearing a cloak with a hood, and by her figure he felt sure it was Angela. She kept near the wall until she had reached the end of the building, when her footsteps took her in the direction of the garden where she was partially hidden by a cypress hedge. Only glimpses of her could he see until she neared the greenhouse where he lost sight of her altogether. Nigel felt he should find out why she should be going out now, but he could not walk about other people's property in the dead of night. He would sit tight and await her return. This occurred within ten minutes, but this time she was not alone.

A tall man was walking back with her. It was impossible

to see his features. They stood for a while talking near the wall of the building and then shook hands as they parted, the man returning through the gardens while Angela walked towards the door. It was at that moment that Nigel was in luck, for the clouds had parted and with a sudden burst of light the moon revealed that the figure was not Angela but was Matilda. Nigel now realized it had been Matilda all along. Should he speak to her in the morning? He was not certain. Also, at last he was feeling tired, so leaving it to his subconscious to look for the solution, he climbed into his bed where within minutes he was asleep.

Nigel awoke very early the next day with fifty per cent of his problems solved. He felt a new man, after all the frustration of collecting masses of clues which did not connect. But now several did, and although it was a risk he had no hesitation with the pre-arranged plans to close this long drawn-out case. He had not solved the midnight perambulations of Matilda, but no doubt this would fall into place. The telephone by his bedside looked inviting but he decided not to use it. So it was half an hour later, when he had left the premises, that he telephoned Scotland Yard and arranged with the Commissioner the formulation of plans for the final swoop.

That afternoon everything was in order for the arrest of the instigators of the deutschmarks robbery from the security van. The Commissioner had approved Nigel's scheme, but first Nigel had to visit the police in Hamburg where he would be staying for a fortnight, while John would be asked to act on his behalf in England. The Home Secretary had been informed that all was ready and he was helping in the arrangements which John had discussed with Nigel many weeks' before.

Nigel returned to his chambers, telling his secretary, George, that should anybody want him he was to tell them that he was still on vacation, and any letters received which required immediate attention should be ignored until he returned.

'The affair I am dealing with now is too big to be sidetracked. So enjoy your holiday, as I know I shall. I will be going to Notley tomorrow and then on to Hamburg, where I shall be staying until this whole business is over.'

Nigel's visit to Notley lasted just one hour, when he proceeded to Gatwick for the flight to Hamburg. His first action on arriving at the Bingham Hotel was to phone John and tell him that he was to represent him at room 243. The Commissioner would let him know the date, which should be in about a week's time. Next he went to the special investigation department of the Hamburg police, where he was given further information about the 12 million deutschmarks robbery.

Returning to his hotel he now had the task of sifting through all his notes, finding other items which now began to fit together like a jigsaw. He found great satisfaction in seeing a picture beginning to take shape. He had nothing else to do now but to await events, so for the next few days he would do just as he had told George he was going to; enjoy his holiday. And what better way could he spend it than visiting Hamburg's famous zoo? And that is precisely what he did.

# 12

Room 243 had the doors firmly closed. Inside the Commissioner had assembled the members of the special branch who had been investigating the West German problem of their security van robbery.

After they were settled he said, 'We hope to see the conclusions of your work in the next few days. It has been one of the most difficult we have had to deal with in recent years. Nigel Danton has provided us with sufficient evidence for me to call this meeting today. He is busy elsewhere but is represented by his colleague John Royston.

'As you know, certain people were suspected of being connected with these robberies, and as they are in this country it has been found necessary to apply for permission to extradite them to face trial in West Germany. These have already been prepared by the Home Secretary. I will hand these to Superintendent Jack Markham, our Notley man whom you all know, and with whom I will have a special word after the meeting. He will be responsible for the final act in this drama; he is shortly to retire, so this should be his crowning achievement, for I know he has been most assiduous in his attention to the details.'

Jack Markham half rose in acknowledgement of this tribute.

The Commissioner now continued at a slower pace, making every word have full effect. 'Now everything will be left in Jack's hands. He will act as soon as he has received Nigel Danton's word to go ahead.'

The Commissioner now addressed himself to Markham, and looking directly at him said, 'You will then take a male and female officer with you. You may choose any who are in this room now. That only leaves me to pass this envelope to you which contains, amongst other things, the Home Secretary's signed extradition order. I want you to read the instructions, Jack, which must be left here; the extradition orders you will keep.'

The superintendent seemed puzzled at being invited to take the responsibility to make the arrests, but consoled himself with the thought that he was allowed to choose the officers to assist him.

The meeting broke up with Jack Markham studying the note which he had to memorize. At last satisfied he had learnt all the information, he passed the envelope back to the Commissioner, while placing the extradition orders in his wallet. The Commissioner then rose from his chair wishing him good luck, and further adding, 'This is not an enviable action you have to perform so I hope it goes smoothly.'

Jack Markham returned to Notley to await Nigel Danton's message.

Belvoir Castle grounds were gay with bunting as the fair and gymkhana began to attract the crowds of visitors for what was going to prove a happy bank holiday for many of them. There had been a little rain early that morning which had now cleared. The sun had risen in a now clear blue sky. Marquees had been erected just inside the gates leading to the park, and it was here that floral exhibits had been arranged. Several of the riders had gathered to admire the tableau of pictures by the different flowers as if they were a carpet suspended along the sides of tents by wires, so that the stems of the flowers could be inserted into little receptacles containing water, whih were well-concealed from the front.

It was amongst these early arrivals that Angela and Clarence had joined to admire and enjoy the perfumes of the flowers while waiting for the horse trials to commence, in which they were both competing. They had travelled from Notley the previous day and joined others staying at Beau Manor, the home of Eugenie Toynbee, a Countess who had retired from France and was now living a few miles away in the village of Hathern. Other guests staying at the manor were the Baron and Baroness Von Ropner, Lady Dalsworth with her personal maid Olive, and Angela's companion Matilda.

The Countess Eugenie had organised them into a party and they had arrived at Belvoir Castle in a big estate car in which extra seats had been fitted. Crowds were now arriving in large numbers coming from as far away as Nottingham and Leicester with special buses from the town of Loughborough. The cars and coaches were accommodated on the lower paddock where they gradually covered the grass like ink spilling on to green blotting paper, until all but a small section was covered by the time the festivities were due to begin. It was at this point that a voice through a loud-hailer from the balcony of the castle told the huge crowd to look up at the sky to observe the arrival of geese from Scandinavia, which came at this time of the year to spend their winter on the lake in the park. This was a phenomenal sight, as they wheeled in perfect formation before alighting on the lake.

From then, other attractions occupied everyone in the carnival atmosphere, to be followed by the judging of various events, before the horse trials commenced. This was a long process, with the judges riding each horse in turns. Then came the jumps in which the Baron again took the trophy, while Clarence and Angela could get nowhere near the winners, although they had good horses. Their riding was not up to their usual standard, and they looked disappointed as they joined the Countess's group, who were seated in the tea tent where a table had been set aside for them. The Baron was the next to arrive, with his trophy and looking very pleased, while the Baroness remarked, 'Another ostrich egg cup to go on our mantlepiece.'

They were all still laughing at this little pleasantry when Superintendent Jack Markham, accompanied by two other officers, one of whom was female, approached the group.

Markham gave a rather stiff bow to Lady Dalsworth, saying, 'I regret we have some very unpleasant business to perform,' and without hesitating said, as he turned to

134

Clarence and Angela, 'It is my duty to detain you both in connection with robberies which have occurred in West Germany while you were there, and I must further add that anything you might say now will be taken down and used in evidence.'

Lady Dalsworth looked horrified, and turned away, while Clarence and Angela looked absolutely bewildered. At last Clarence said, 'You mean to arrest us now, here?'

'That is so,' replied Markham. 'It will be better this way. We have a conveyance waiting outside.'

The policewoman moved towards Angela, who stood perfectly still when a hand was placed on her arm.

The Countess said, 'As my guests I will not allow you to be exposed like this to idle onlookers; let us all go to your conveyance together. It will be less conspicuous and embarrassing for you both.'

So the party moved to the gates where Clarence and Angela allowed themselves to be placed in a police car.

Clarence turned to his mother, saying, 'Contact our solicitor, mother, and our apologies to you, Countess Eugenie, for causing you this embarrassment.'

The Countess made no reply but looked down as if deep in thought.

'May I ask,' enquired Lady Dalsworth, 'where you are taking them?'

'All I am allowed to say, m'Lady,' Markham was now very formal, 'is to advise you that they will be taken to Scotland Yard where they will stay the night before travelling to Hamburg tomorrow to face charges. That is all I am at liberty to say. Although I will add that you will be able to obtain any further information the authorities are likely to disclose at your local police station.'

He turned, entering the police car which quickly drove away from the group and a small bunch of curious bystanders.

Countess Eugenie said, 'We must not upset ourselves over this. Come, let us all return to the manor.'

The prisoners, meanwhile, sat silent as the car sped along the motorway to London, where three hours' later they arrived to be placed in secure apartments inside Scotland Yard.

The Commissioner expressed his appreciation of the method that Markham had adopted to make the arrest. 'Now you have done so well it has only to be concluded by you transporting them to Germany for the West Germans to deal with, so this should be about your last job before retirement.'

He replied that he was just about all-in, as the work these last few months had been very strenuous, so that if anybody else could be spared for the rest of the journey he would prefer that.

'I quite understand, Jack, but the extradition order is very explicit about who should hand them over, and the name Jack Markham has been forwarded to Hamburg. So I'm afraid it's just a little more, Jack, and then you can look forward to the retirement you have earned.'

The flight to Hamburg the next day was by a special police plane containing five passengers: Clarence and Angela escorted by Markham and the two police officers. The one looking after Angela gave her all her attention as she was showing considerable distress.

Upon arrival at the police headquarters in Hamburg, all five were ushered into a small reception room, where they sat awaiting their fate. Jack Markham told his officers to stay close to the prisoners while he went to seek the officer who would then charge them in accordance with German regulations.

He returned in five minutes with the officer and two policemen. After telling them to stand, the officer asked Markham for the extradition papers which, when handed over, he read very slowly. He then looked very hard at Angela and Clarence, saying, 'Neither of you look at all well. I think you should be taken out into the air.'

He motioned their escorting officers to take their arms while one of the German policemen opened a side door for them. As they left the room, Clarence half turned to see Markham and the officer facing each other. The officer was holding up the extradition papers and deliberately tearing them in half.

Still being ushered along a corridor they at last reached an outside door which led down four steps to the pavement. A car was drawn up at that point and their

136

escorts were now smiling, for on reaching the car they were astounded to see Nigel step from it, saying, 'Welcome back from the jaws of whatever it was; we are all now going back to Blighty. Sorry we had to put you to all this trouble. It was the only way.'

Angela said, 'I had a vibe about it all, and felt as if I was playing a part in some Victorian melodrama.'

'You certainly had me guessing,' said her escort. 'I thought you were going to do a real faint.'

'I did my best,' agreed Angela.

The plane was still waiting for them to make the return trip while Clarence kept saying, 'By jove, whoever would have thought it after all the hospitality we have given to Jack Markham?'

'Yes, you are right,' said Nigel. 'You have assumed correctly that he was the one they wanted back, and this was the only way it could be done without a lot of publicity. You see, it would create a very bad image to have a long-serving super extradited to a foreign country, but as it is he has gone freely and must answer for his conduct in a country he has abused. I know I should not prejudge, but the evidence against him he will find is watertight.'

Clarence said, 'I noticed we had no trouble with our passports.'

'Quite so. Immigration and passport control were all aware of your flight and the two governments made it very easy.'

They parted at Gatwick, Angela and Clarence being met by the family chauffeur for the unescorted journey back to Lynton Hall.

A police car was waiting for Nigel and the two officers, who left him at his chambers while they continued to Scotland Yard to make out their reports.

John Royston was waiting for Nigel with a whisky ready for him as he entered.

'Ah, just what I need,' said Nigel as he sipped the Johnny Walker.

'Me too,' said John. 'So I suppose we can drink to a successful end to the case?'

'Yes, it's been a tricky one, a very tricky one. At one stage I did not know whether I was coming or going.'

'So,' said John, 'as I have not been in on it very much I'm interested in what you have been up to and how you arrived at the answer.'

Nigel settled back in his chair and placed his hands together, while looking in deep thought before commencing to speak.

'The answer is, I discovered the first inkling of who was responsible when I last went to dinner at Lynton Hall, when you were invited but could not go. Now, Fraulein Henkel, who was Angela's old tutor on India and who I got to know as Matilda, told a story at the dinner; it was for children, but as the Baron Ropner remarked afterwards, he felt sure it was meant to convey a message. It was this which gave me a lead the next day. Her story was about a schoolboy who had rough treatment because he was left-handed. Then I remembered Joan Markham, the super's wife, was using her left hand at dinner. Also I noticed she had an enlarged joint on her right foot which distorted the shoe, and this was the impression which was made on the moist soil inside the hut on the Ropner estate where the Baron took a tumble.

'I was able to get a group photograph from Lady Dalsworth in which the super and his wife were very clear. This I took to Luneburg where the daughter of the post office keeper recognised both of them; also I remember when I was at the gymkhana held there I noticed some of the men in the high jump ran up to the jump from the left and others from the right, the reason being that most left-handed people are also left-footed and that foot goes over the jump first. Conversely, right-handed people jump with the right foot first. It was the girl at the post office who noticed the woman had a bunion on her right foot as she stepped into the car, because that was the one on the ground last. Also, a day or two before, a shoeman had fitted riding boots on a woman who had a big joint on her right foot. This all happened at Luneburg you understand, John?'

John nodded his head.

'I realized then that they were working together to pin a petty crime on to the others, and that would most likely be Angela and Clarence – hence the purchasing of riding

138

boots to smudge their own presence there. It would seem that Joan Markham had developed a considerable dislike for Angela, as she had usurped Lady Dalsworth's interest away from the Institute at Notley, of which they were both active members. That was the reason she had her husband take a shot at her from the seclusion of the gamekeeper's hut.'

John interrupted to ask, 'Why, when they had secured eight million or so in marks, should they take such a risk as to stage a robbery for just a few, and then leave themselves open to being arrested by shooting at the riders when so many onlookers were about?'

'Yes, John, I can understand you asking that question. It is one which I have asked myself many times. On my last visit to Notley before going to Hamburg I saw the doctor who had attended Markham. He told me that Joan Markham was a very strange woman who had an almost hypnotic effect on him when she forestalled him from seeing her husband, and her insistence on supplying him with flowers and cuttings, knowing that the doctor was a keen gardener. He realized her powers of coercion were strong and this was no doubt the power she exerted on her husband which brought about their undoing.

'If you remember, when we first met the Commissioner in Scotland Yard he told us that Markham had the flu at the time of the two hold-ups in West Germany, and the doctor had visited him every day. This was not strictly true. The doctor had visited the house every day and had only seen Joan Markham, who had said her husband felt better and had gone horse riding in order to get the air.

'I later found out that Markham was an excellent shot, who one year was third at Bisley. After I had examined the hut with Baron Ropner I went back alone by taking the car to the other side of the woods, and saw car tracks and the same boot impressions on the turf, so they could have easily rejoined the crowds. It was then that Lady Dalsworth saw them and was affected by doing so.

'My contention is that he was in West Germany when we went to Hamburg. The two Dalsworths were there, also Matilda, and he hoped to throw suspicion on them but was forestalled by a rival gang who nearly got rid of us while waiting for the Englishman, who was undoubtedly Markham. Had he met us then our deaths would have been certain. That was a period when he and his wife were supposed to have been on holiday. I feel Lady Dalsworth may have communicated her feelings to her children about her mistrust of Markham, for when I come to think of it, when I last went to Lynton Hall and Angela gave an encore at the dinner evening she played *The Sorcerers Apprentice*. I wonder if that had any significance? Also, when they both came out of the police station at Hamburg they were both very cool. When speaking to her police escort, Angela spoke of putting on an act about almost fainting, saying she felt she was acting in a Victorian melodrama. Yes, I think they had very strong suspicions, but fortunately they did nothing to frighten Markham from proceeding to the final curtain.'

'What about the extradition papers?' asked John.

'There were none,' Nigel replied. 'They could not have been issued like that. It was an entire hoax. I don't suppose you have seen extraditon orders. Nor have I. And I am sure Markham had not done so either. What he took with him looked very official, and you may be sure the Commissioner would make him feel they were very precious. The Home Secretary knew of the arrangement and that was all; it was risky but it worked.'

At that moment the telephone rang. It was the Commissioner saying, 'It's all wrapped up, Nigel. Our special branch have visited Joan Markham in Notley, and she has signed a full statement of these activities. It seems they had tried to copy the Manipulator's activities to make a very quick fortune, and of course they had the local information to help them. The money had been put in a Swiss bank and she has given us the numbers of the accounts. She and her husband had planned to move abroad in a week's time, not Bournemouth after all. West Germany is making no charges against her, although we should have had to do so if Markham had pleased her by hitting Miss Dalsworth with a pistol shot. So that's that. West Germany have been informed and are happy.

'Not very good for us to have a respected old member of the force to turn crooked, but there it is. Time will heal the wound to our pride. Your cheque will be along in a day or so. Until the next time, keep yourself fit.'

The Commissioner had said his piece, and the case was closed.

Three weeks' later Markham was convicted of organising a gang in West Germany to rob security vans. The first was of US notes, the value of which was not disclosed and never recovered. From the second robbery of twelve million deutschmarks, ten million were traced to a Swiss bank and returned to their rightful owners.

Markham was sentenced to twelve years' imprisonment. No charges were made against his wife as they considered she had been coerced into assisting him. Full reports were made in all the West German newspapers, while the Hamburg daily press headed their contribution as 'the Manipulator's disciples'. Whether this included the wife was not clear.

Nigel and George had again started work after the summer recess, and were sorting out the morning mail when the telephone rang. George picked it up, saying, 'It's for you,' as he handed it to Nigel.

He was surprised to hear the same voice of many months ago which had suggested he should visit his dentist. Nigel had thought little of Angela since she had given him that cold, far-away look at the dinner party.

George noticed a colouring up of Nigel's cheeks, in spite of his holiday tan, as he answered, saying he was well and also his friend John, which was the reply to her next question. Then there was a considerable delay until the voice said, 'Lady Ursula would like to know if you and your friend would care to call and see us. Would next Tuesday be convenient?'

Thank you. I know I can get John to come along this time.'

'Thank you,' replied that soft, silken voice. 'We shall be looking forward to seeing you.'

Nigel looked across at George, whose attention was still concerned with the letters. He hoped his voice or looks would not betray the pleasure he felt.

The next day he telephoned John and was surprised to hear that Lady Dalsworth had discovered their number and had asked that Margaret should join them, saying, 'We shall be having a little music, after which we hope you will be able to stay the night. And please ask your friend, Nigel, if he would care to stay also.'

Nigel met John and Margaret at Euston Station and soon they had cleared the London traffic and were on the road to Sussex. The weather was warm and the sky clear of clouds. He did not wish to speak but to whistle and hum pleasant tunes along the way. John would still keep speaking of the robberies, to which he had no option but to reply, especially as Margaret was in the back seat supposedly reading a magazine in between watching the passing scenes of the countryside.

'One thing you haven't explained,' persisted John. 'When you were here last time and saw Matilda walk out at midnight across the lawn where she met somebody who walked back with her to the house – can you tell me what that was about?'

Nigel replied, 'Yes, I remember. When I went to the hospital I noticed they had an Indian doctor there; as you know, Matilda has spent many years in India and I heard them speaking together in a language which was neither English or German. I do not think that had any bearing on the case, but was just an attraction between two people who could share a common interest.'

It was five o'clock when they arrived at Lynton Hall, and were immediately taken to their room by a footman who said that the others were assembled in the music room for a short musical recital by Miss Angela.

'It will be commencing in a quarter of an hour,' he added.

They were mystified by this reception, but on their entry into the music room they were greeted by clapping from the few assembled there. Lady Dalsworth was standing just inside and Margaret was introduced to her before they took their seats. Angela was already at the piano, with Clarence next to her to adjust the pages of music. The Baron and Baroness were also present, as was the Countess Eugenie Toynbee, which surprised Nigel in view of the disappointment to her day at Belvoir Castle. Matilda was sitting a little apart and speaking to the vicar, both of them looking extremely happy, while Angela was decidedly nervous as she commenced to play, striking a few wrong notes and not giving the pedals their full use. Although her music became faultless as she continued, it lacked the usual expression which she had previously employed. The music finished with the usual show of appreciation as Angela stepped down from the dais to go to Matilda's side of the room where she stood perfectly still.

Lady Dalsworth now stood, saying, 'Will you all now please stand.'

Angela turned and went behind a curtain which had been placed against an open door, and reappeared pushing a wheelchair containing none other than Thomas Atkins, who she brought further into the room until he was in the centre by the piano.

Lady Dalsworth said, 'We placed the curtain there so that Thomas could hear the music and he did not wish to embarrass you. But now he will tell you a story which I know will astound all of you. As you can see, he has made a very remarkable recovery and it is anticipated within a few weeks he will no longer require the wheelchair.'

During the clapping which followed, Clarence placed a seat next to Thomas which Angela now accepted.

When the applause had subsided, Thomas Atkins commenced his story. He thanked Lady Dalsworth for this opportunity to bare his soul amongst such illustrious company, in such a relaxed setting of this fine building, 'Parts of which I am well-acquainted with,' he added with a smile.

'My story begins way back in India where my parents took me when I was ten years of age. They had moved there from England when my father obtained a position as a tea planter. I grew up on the plantation and eventually assisted with the processing of the tea and the exporting documents, also the wages for the field staff. When I was thirty years of age I fell in love with the daughter of a tea planter further along the hills. She was ten years younger then me and we were ideally happy. Nothing, it seemed, could alter.

'But one afternoon, when her parents were visiting us

with their daughter, Mary, and we were sitting outside watching the sky as it was lit up that evening by lightning far away over the mountains, there was a sound of an enormous explosion and her father said, "My God, the dam has burst up in the hills!"

'In no time we could see the wall of water moving in our direction. Then we realized our only hope of escape was to cross the ravine by the only rope bridge near our house. We let our parents go first; my father had not been well for some years and they could not hurry across. We stood and watched them as the bridge started to swing in the wind. They had reached about half way across when the rope bridge swung over itself like a child's skipping rope and then snapped, throwing all four into the fearsome cascade four hundred feet below, to be lost forever.'

Thomas Atkins stopped speaking while Angela gave him a glass of wine. Having taken two sips he returned it to her before continuing in a stronger voice.

'We both looked down into what was a boiling cauldron, but to me it appeared the depths of hell itself. We were marooned, with the water now rushing towards us. The noise was fearful as all our tea and the plants were washed along in its path. We saw people young and old. Some were screaming while others were now just dead bodies floating amongst them, being twisted and turned in that turbulent water which was now turning to our left before cascading into the chasm where our parents had gone.

'The storm which we had been watching over the mountains now burst overhead. The lightning was continuous, while the crashing of the rocks, trees and soil over the edge, to fall all that distance below, was sufficiently great as to mask any sound of thunder. It was a Niagara of water, rocks and trees, and alas, humans.

'We were powerless to save anybody as we stood petrified with fear for I don't know how many hours as the avalanche continued. When daylilght came we could see the water was subsiding and the devastation was complete; our house had gone and our plantation was now plain soil. It was as if a giant razor had scraped the face of the earth for as far as we could see. Even my young lady's home and plantation which was two miles' away had suffered the same fate. We were ruined and we knew it. We started walking, often sinking to our knees in mud, but eventually reached dry land and found refuge in a hut where we both fell to the floor on the earth and slept.'

'I awoke first, and although still exhausted opened the door and saw some people on horseback who had come looking in that vast expanse, which looked more like a desert now that the sun was drying everything. They saw me and called out; we were then lifted on to the horses and taken to a village ten miles' away. It was then that I would have to begin a new career again. Fortunately it was a progressive village which would soon grow into a town, for a copper mine was being opened up and men were arriving to work there.

'I had found work with a builder, and it was then that we decided to get married. I found the work hard as I helped with loading the rocks; eventually I learnt a bit about the dressing of the stones, and when they found I was adept they encouraged me until I had mastered the carving of the stonework and became their mason. Things were now improving and I was able to build our house, so from then on we started to take an interest in other matters as we tried to conceal the pain of the loss of our parents.

'It was about this time that troops came to the village; it was winter now and there had been a particularly heavy fall of snow and later flooding. But it did not come near our village, which had grown to a small town and was called Patna.

'It was as the floods started to go that some of the soldiers became ill. A few died while others became delirious with sickness and malaria fever. One soldier was very ill and he was left when the regiment left; two Sepoys stayed behind to care for him. One I did not like at all, and as the soldier was an Englishman I used to go and talk to him during his lucid moments until he was sufficiently well to travel down to the plains where he could rejoin his regiment.'

Thomas was perspiring a little and Angela passed a glass of water to him, which he now took more freely. After a few moments he continued, 'When the soldiers left life became more normal, except that the copper mine was not yielding as well as expected, so less and less men were employed. I was fortunate to keep my job but there was not a lot of building so that my income suffered. We managed very well, with care, and awaited better times. Month by month our savings dwindled as we waited for the regiment to return, and this time they required a permanent fort to be built. This provided me with more work than I could manage. Before it was completed they had to go to the assistance of another regiment who had been in a skirmish with rebels in the hills.

'It was at this time that my wife gave birth to a girl. She was the image of her mother, and it was while we were sitting one evening in front of our wood fire while the baby lay cooing in the cot that we heard a knock on the side window. I looked up, thinking it was a bough tapping against the glass, but to my surprise I saw that it was one of the Sepoys who had been left to look after the Englishman some three years' before.

'I went to the door and brought him inside. He was cold so I made him a hot drink fortified with spirits brewed in the town. My wife was not alarmed when he came in as he was the gentle one. I asked after his companion, and to this he said that was why he was here. He told me he had been killed in the recent skirmish and he had collected his effects which he did not know what to do with. There were no dependants that he could hand them to, and although he utterly disliked the other Sepoy, who he suspected was mixed up in some kind of shady deal, he would not wish the regiment to know what he had been doing, so he hoped I would take the things which he would not be returning to the regiment.

'I said to him, "Isn't it an offence not to return all his belongings to them?"

'He replied, "I don't think you will say so when you see what he has been doing. Although my reading of English is not good, I've seen enough not to let the regiment know; in any case, our company is being disbanded in a fortnight and then all left-overs are burnt."

'"Very good," I said, "let me have them if it makes you feel any better."

146

'He then handed over to me a small packet which he seemed mighty relieved to part with.

'"Thanks," he said. "I did not like him but I would not like his memory to be besmirched. After all, he was a good fighter and in a fortnight's time all will be forgotten."

'He looked at his watch, saying, "I must go, but just one thing more. I've hesitated to mention it, but when the Englishman was in delirium he thought he had an affair with a native woman, which he didn't. When he recovered my rogue of a partner went to find him and told him the woman had had a baby and said he would report him, so started to blackmail him. But it's all in the book where he kept his records. Now I must go, so I don't expect I shall see you again. Fine baby you have there."

'This caused my wife to look up with a smile as he went out. That was the last I saw of him.

'The story was a nasty one. Just to think of the agony that Englishman must have suffered. I put the packet away undisturbed. It was not meant for me, and if anyone from the army asked about it I could just hand it over claiming ignorance as to its contents. But nobody came. The regiment was disbanded and I thought no more about it until an epidemic hit the place once more. Many people died, and I found myself a widower.

'My daughter was now four and a half years of age and I was at my wit's end to think how I could cope. Then I remembered the packet the Sepoy had given me. When I opened it I saw that what the Sepoy had told me was correct. The Englishman had been well and truly hood-winked, and thought he was sending his daughter to a school for the children of gentlefolk, when the blackguard had been taking the money for himself.

'The affairs of the Englishman did not make good reading. It seemed he had been making money from hospital supplies; not that he had kept the hospitals short – he had in fact been over-ordering. He had then sold the surplus to other private hospitals. The Sepoy knew this and kept pressure on him, so it must have been a great relief when he found he was not being blackmailed. I read more of the notes and saw the child who never was had been named Angela Dalsworth, and was supposedly sent

147

to a school in Cawnpore.'

There were several sharp intakes of breath in the room, while Angela was looking down almost in tears.

He continued, 'I knew then what I could do to ensure a future for my child and relieve me of the distress it would cause us both if I tried to manage alone in a native village with no other English children with whom she could become friends. Also, I was sure she would not survive another winter in these hills without a mother's care. I would have to travel quite a lot, being away for weeks at a time; there was only one thing I could do, and that was to have my girl renamed Angela and take her to the school in Cawnpore. In preparation for this I kept calling my daughter Angela instead of Mary, which was her mother's name, but as we more often called her dear or darling she soon got used to her new name.

'I found out that the school did exist. The Sepoy was clever enough to give a real one and not a fictitious one. In the packet were cheques made out to bearer, which had come from Clarence Dalsworth; why they had not been cashed was a mystery, until I found a piece of paper showing he had an obscure bank in Calcutta which would not have had the facilities for banking at other banks, so he would have to keep them until he visited Calcutta; they were safer than cash in a regiment. I'm sure the other Sepoy did not realize their true worth, which when I added them up came to over two thousand rupees.

'I changed some of the cheques at a local bank and dressed my little daughter in fine clothes, and also bought a new suit made by a local tailor for myself, and spent more money travelling down to the plains where we stayed overnight at Delhi, then by train to Cawnpore where I found no difficulty in finding the school for young ladies of gentlefolk.

'We took a cab from the station, and I left Angela in it while I made enquiries to see if she could be accepted. I passed myself off as Clarence Dalsworth, saying I had come from Delhi, and wished to place my daughter in the care of that school which had such a splendid reputation. I explained that I would shortly be leaving the country but funds would always be made available for her education.'

148

Thomas looked across at Matilda. 'Do you remember?' he asked.

'Yes,' she answered. 'I remember very well indeed.'

'She then asked me if she could see the child. When I brought her in, dressed in all her new clothes, I knew that she had made a conquest. I offered the remainder of the cheques of about eleven hundred rupees, saying other cheques would be forthcoming from Delhi at regular intervals.

'Matilda agreed to take Angela so I returned to the car and collected the new case containing other clothing for my girl. I hurried away, not daring to look back, not stopping at Delhi. But at the station I hired a cab for my return home.

'My task was to write a letter to Clarence Dalsworth informing him that owing to the death of the Sepoy who was caring for his daughter at a private school it would be more practical to send monies direct to Fraulein Henkel, the Headmistress.

'From then on I lived alone, travelling around the doing jobs of any description, knowing I had done what I considered best at that time for my little daughter. I could not dare return to see her at the school in case the real Lord Dalsworth had been there, when my deception would have been exposed.

Many years later I read that Lord Dalsworth had died, and that his widow was coming to India for a brief visit. The rest you can guess. I was able to trace her movements (sorry my Lady), and find out where she would be going, and that is how I discovered my daughter was living. From then on all I wanted to do was to watch her progress, so I followed you both back to England and obtained work at the Hall. It was then that I began to notice the attraction which was developing between Angela and Clarence, or I should say Lord Clarence. I knew how they must have been tearing their hearts out, so now I hope this will put the matter right, as I am able.'

He then felt in his pocket and produced his marriage certificate, also Angela's birth certificate. The name Mary had been changed, and the alteration had been signed and dated.

149

Angela rose and kissed her father. Lady Dalsworth's eyes were full of tears, while Nigel's eyes were moist as he realized he would never get any closer to Angela than he was tonight. Yet in his heart he was aware her future was in a realm far removed from his own.

Thomas Atkins then said, 'So now we have an Angela Atkins, who should be about two years younger than yourself, Clarence.'

'Quite right, Thomas,' Clarence replied. 'And that I cannot alter, but the name I can.'

He stepped across to Angela and, holding her gently, kissed her. Then, turning to his mother, he said, 'Mother, we are engaged.'

Congratulations followed from them all, Matilda saying, 'I knew the night when we all had dinner together here, but I was not absolutely sure until the doctor told me. I had to meet him when you had all retired because Thomas had recovered his speech and the doctor wished to tell me things, which he thought I was the best one to tell the rest of the family. I informed Lady Ursula, and now you all know. Countess Eugenie Toynbee said she felt all along that they were meant for each other.'

At that moment the footman opened the doors to the dining-room, saying dinner was served. Lady Dalsworth stepped next to Nigel, saying, 'Shall we lead them in?'

'Certainly, m'Lady,' he replied.

'Certainly, Ursula,' she said with a smile as she placed her hand very lightly on his left arm.

# 13

Jack Markham was in solitary confinement. He had been well treated and was not feeling lonely, for he had plenty to think about; his cell was at the end of a corridor from the main block, away from the other inmates of this top security prison, far removed from any town or village.

His police training gave him time to reflect on his condition and situation, similar to that which he had been instrumental in imposing on so many others. But he was now a criminal; he had no authority, for this had been stripped from him by his own actions.

He knew now he should never have given way to his wife's wishes that he should try and shoot at Angela Dalsworth as she rode by in the race on the Baron Ropner's estate. Good a shot as he was, he knew he would never have been certain of hitting anything but the horse, which would have in all likelihood caused the rider to tumble, the result of which he hoped would not have caused serious harm to the rider but would have pacified Joan. The wrong rider had been made to fall, with the result that he was now in his present plight. In a self-critical mood he allowed his face to crease in the semblance of a smile as his lips silently moved to the words, 'Hoist with his own petard.'

He must now await the interview, which he knew as a freshman would be his lot with the prison governor before he was allowed to join the other prisoners. What a thought. And what prospect would he have of being able to serve his term of twelve years without molestation from the inmates, who would know of his police duties? They would try all in their power to cause him to retaliate and lose any remission from his sentence, which he had no intention of serving.

Yes, he would use all his knowledge of the criminal code, of which he had a lifetime's experience, to escape from West Germany. Joan had divulged numbers of the Swiss account to Scotland Yard, but the two million unaccounted for both he and she knew was still safe in a bank in Basle.

Joan had played her part well, and remaining free she could make the necessary arrangements for his departure from wherever the authorities had him confined. It was only a matter of time before he would be allowed to write to her, and she had the numbers which would enable her to read his letter in the context that would convey a message. Joan was clever. She would use the information to do just as he wished.

He looked around his cell and found no comfort in his immediate surroundings, with its wooden bunk-bed, one blanket, one slop pail and one bench fixed to the wall, a high window with vertical steel bars. There was no water; he had to wait for this to be delivered. His morning sluice was at the pump in the small compound outside, where a prison officer stood fully armed while he washed and shaved with the cold water, after which he had to place his shaving tackle on a nearby shelf before returning to his quarters, where he was allowed to keep the towel for ten minutes, which then had to be passed through a small opening in the cell door from where he was observed from time to time. One thing they could not do, that was to see into his mind.

It was about a month later that he was summoned to the Governor's office. His shaving soap and razor were on a desk behind which sat the Governor, whom he estimated was about fifty years of age. He was quite thin, not the accepted idea of a thick-necked Prussian officer. His features were aristocratic, while his hands, which he held together on the desk, were as thin as those of an artist or musician. His eyes, as he gazed at Markham, were cold ice-blue, but this made little impression as Jack Markham had adopted a similar attitude in the past to impress and perhaps quail a likely suspect. The two escorts stood either side of him, looking straight ahead, perhaps not wishing to catch the eye of the Governor, who spoke after a moment's silence.

'We are sending you to another prison where you will be given work to do for which we feel you are best fitted.'

The guard on Markham's right gave a slight cough and was immediately silenced by a sharp exclamation and a stab from the icy blue eyes of the Governor, who turned his attention back to Markham.

'You will be working with other prisoners, and it will be up to you how you respond to their company. You understand?'

A nod was all he received in response.

Early the next morning while it was still dark, being late October, he was called out of his cell, given his shaving things and told to follow a guard while another walked behind him with a pistol, prodding him in an effort to keep up with the striding guard who led them through a gate in the high brick wall where three other prisoners were waiting. All four were ordered into a police van. Markham noticed the other prisoners had the look of lifers who had lost all interest in expression, sitting dolefully while a chain fitted to the inside of the van was encircled around their waists. Markham, having taken up a position on the floor, was also treated likewise.

The van had an open top. In fact it could be described as a lorry, except that special provision had been made for seats for the two armed guards who had their portion roofed as a special protection from the weather. A brief word from an officer at the gate and the vehicle moved away with a police car following.

Jack Markham looked at his fellow passengers who neither spoke to each other nor intimated they had seen him come aboard. If they were all going to the same place then they had twelve years in which to get to know him. All he was concerned about was the prospect of being confined for the period of his sentence. So he, like the others, remained silent as the police van and its escort left the district, travelling the main highway at increasing speed going south. After about an hour they left this good road for one which was in very poor condition, and being deeply rutted and stony made their position extremely uncomfortable. However, after a short while they stopped at a deserted stretch of countryside, where the guards unchained the prisoners, telling them they could relieve themselves then wash and shave by a drinking fountain at the roadside before they were again secured as before when the journey continued.

Jack Markham noticed they had passed signposts to Brunswick and then Halberstadt before they stopped for food which consisted of bread, cheese and tomato washed down with fresh milk that was brought from the boot of the escort car. The guards had a similar fare, but their beverage was larger for which they had china mugs that were constantly being refilled from a barrel also kept in the boot.

The meal being over, they were informed by one of the guards that they would be arriving at their new home late in the afternoon, so no further stops would be made. The journey continued as before but over very hilly country, until they came to the town of Gotha, after which the road was again rough but also twisted and turned, making the prisoners grasp on to each other or their chains in order to remain in an upright position. It must have been after a half hour of this torture that they arrived at the new top security prison, situated well away, as was the previous one, from any form of private habitation; not even a solitary cottage, over an expanse of countryside dominated by the prison complex which was encompassed by fencing two miles distant from it, and not a tree or shrub between.

The road finished at a wire fence which Markham noticed was electrified and also barbed, providing an additional restrainer to another set further back and which would no doubt be similarly constructed, while the space between them could be mined or some other device arranged.

The prisoners from the van were now made to enter a gate which was manned by about a dozen guards with automatic weapons, while the van and escort returned to another road which led to the prison proper, while they were compelled to walk the two miles to the buildings.

Markham felt this was a miserable piece of gamesmanship which was unreasonable unless it was to reduce their spirits even further.

Having arrived and been checked in, Jack found himself again in a cell to himself, but high up in the building which provided him with a view where he could observe the comings and going of prisoners and the various activities in which they were engaged.

After another week in solitary he was escorted to the Governor's office. He was invited to stand in a box-like device which they called the dock, and from where he was informed he would be questioned as to his capabilities before being given work with the other prisoners. The Governor was entirely different from the previous one he had seen. This one was a man of a heavy build, and his moon face gave no hint of his thoughts as the grey eyes looked steadily at him.

'Now, what I wish to know is your history. So you can tell me all you can remember from your birth.'

The Governor leaned back in his chair behind his desk and carefully polished a monocle. He looked at Jack, who felt he was a rabbit being hypnotised by a stoat.

Jack did not need this treatment and was only too pleased to give them a story, as he had already formulated a plan of escape and would give them an opportunity to humble him, and at the same time give him his wish. And so he fabricated a history, saying when he left school he volunteered for the merchant navy and was taught all the various jobs a seaman must know. This was just the language which started them smiling to each other, the two officers asking questions in turn while the Governor, still leaning on his arms, allowed his face to adopt a benign expression as his monocle fell in his lap.

'How old were you when you joined the navy?' asked one officer, each trying to outdo the other in suggesting he had been a child prodigy. Jack answered their questions with every sign of embarrassment as each inquisitor fired another question.

The Governor intervened to say, 'We do this to try and find out what you are capable of; we do know that as an English policeman you have qualities which you could hardly exercise here, you cannot very well police yourself, and we have plenty who can do just that. What was your other job, shall we say your principal one, on the ship in your early days?'

Jack allowed his eyes to drop at the Governor's steel-grey look. In a very subdued voice he answered, 'I was in charge of the heads.'

There was a short silence followed by laughter from the two officers as the Governor continued speaking. 'So you were head of the heads, I suppose, before you were promoted to the bridge beside the Captain? I think we have just such a position here we can offer you. I doubt very much if you will progress, as one who has the job tends to stick to it, or rather it tends to stick to him until his retirement from here.'

Markham stood looking down at the papers and pencils on the desk, hoping his look of crestfallen despondency would be accepted by his tormentors as genuine. Inwardly he felt he was now well on his way to formulating his plans for escape.

The interview over, the governor recovered his monocle and sat upright watching Markham's departure with two guards who had been called in to usher him off to his quarters. Back in his cell he hoped the task that he would be given would be the one of looking after the latrines, and the disposal of the soil. He had observed that this was accomplished by a single man with his mule and cart, on which the scraping of a shovel even over a mile away could be clearly heard as he cleared the cart at the disposal tip. The prison officers would inspect it on his return and if found unsatisfactory, the journey would have to be repeated.

Markham noted that the cart, pulled by the same old mule and led by the same prisoner, occurred about twice a week. High above the road an armed sentry from his observation tower watched the man, mule and cart every inch of the way there and back.

Several days after Markham had been returned to his cell he was awakened very early one morning and brought his breakfast. Two extra slices were included and he was urged to have a good meal as he was to assist the other

156

prisoner to clean the latrines, 'and you may lose your appetite until you get used to what you have to do.'

# 14

Joan Markham was no longer living at Notley, for she had chosen to live with her monosyllabic sister, Martha, at Christchurch, near Bournemouth. Her last enquiries to the police elicited the reply that her husband had been removed to a prison not too far from Munich, and he would be allowed to write to her, although the letters she must understand would be censored. If her husband wished to communicate she could be sure she would receive the letters.

It was not until six months after Jack's arrest that she received her first letter.

Joan's sister, Martha, who was six years' older than herself, had remained a spinster, having been in service to a clergyman and his wife who both died during an influenza epidemic. Not having any living relations to which their property could be left, Martha found herself the possessor of their large house. It had six bedrooms, so being enterprising she let the rooms to casual visitors, and it soon became known as a boarding house used mostly by commercial travellers who could park their cars on the ample space behind the building. Her income was thus assured, while two local girls provided all the help she wanted. Joan knew her sister was pleased to have her and she paid her for the room. She felt quite at home as she had brought with her some of her own furniture.

Joan had just taken a shower one morning when there was a double tap on the door. Hastily arranging a towel she heard her sister call through the closed door, 'A letter for you.'

She had no need to open the door as a buff envelope

appeared by her bare feet. Joan reached down and picked up the envelope. Her fingers seemed to burn as she noted the stamp was one from West Germany. Taking the envelope to the window she tore it open to read this first communication from her husband.

'My dearest Joan, at last I am able to write to you. Firstly, I hope you are well and to say I am also. I have an interesting job here. I have been given the address of Martha, so I expect you are staying with her as you have told the authorities that is where I can write; which is once every fortnight. There is a considerable number of occupants here, and in my next letter I will be able, I hope, to tell you how many numbers there are. I shall be looking forward to your letters, and I will write to you as soon as permitted. I have fixed a calendar in my cell and cross out the numbers each day. Keep well and give my love to your sis; and to you my sweet, as always, Your devoted Jack.'

Joan read the letter twice before carefully folding it and locking it in the writing desk she had brought with her from Notley. Drying herself quickly, having smelt the bacon and realized her breakfast was ready, she left her room in better spirits than she had experienced for many days. She would write to Jack that morning and would look forward to his next letter in which he had made it clear he would use numbers of which she had a list, but which he carried in his head, so that she would be able to decipher the hidden message. Martha was surprised that Joan had eaten all her breakfast and even more astounded when she was asked for any scraps of bread for Joan to take along to the river bank to feed the swans; not only were the swans to be fed but Joan also took her writing material along with her.

Jack Markham had been employed as latrine assistant for about a month and the jibes which both the guards and prisoners had continually thought up to embarrass him were now fewer as he showed no reaction and their interest in him grew less. He was still subject to the harassment of those he had to please, although his teacher who accompanied him was only too pleased to be rid of the actual work and enjoyed acting as his overseer while Jack did the shovelling of the muck. On reaching the pits

159

the mule would be let out to graze while again the metal-lined cart would have to be emptied and thoroughly cleaned for the inspection of the wardens on their return. No efforts were spared to make his task as unpleasant as possible, for no matter how clean the cart was on his return he would be compelled to get in the cart while his foreman had to spray it with disinfectant, and although Jack tried to avoid the spray it was noticeable that more often than not the spray was directed so that his clothing was saturated with the filth which was thrown up in the process.

He found because of his job he was not popular with any of the other prisoners; not only because of his job but also the fact that he was considered an undesirable alien, not fit to mix with these undesirable natives.

He had cleaned the steel-lined cart one day after he had been given a particularly offensive soaking with the disinfectant, and was just about to fetch the mule for the return trip when his overseer told him that the following week he would be on his own.

'I am leaving,' said his overseer. 'I've finished my time and will be going back to my own job as a barber. I expect you will have a warden with you for a while but you can soon get rid of him; just slop some on his trousers, he won't worry you much after that. Then you will be left alone as long as they hear the shovel going from time to time.

'You won't have to worry about losing your job, the only way that can happen would be if you were ill or died. It will be at the end of your stretch when they will find some other likely cove for you to train, and that's the way it is.'

Jack received this information with an enthusiasm he was at pains to conceal, as he replied in an undertone, 'I shall miss you.'

The mule having been placed between the shafts, they made the return journey in silence, under the ever watchful guard on the tower. All was in order when the inspection was completed and his foreman was not asked to use the hose on the cart.

Jack had been on his own when he received a letter from Joan. It had been opened by the prison censor. He

160

did not wish to read it until the end of the day, hoping it would contain more in it than the obvious clichés. He would restrain his feelings until he was clean and tidy; also the waiting added spice to the anticipation of hoped for good news. So it was after the evening meal when he was confined to his cell that he commenced to read.

'My Darling Husband, I was delighted to receive your letter and to know you are well and have something interesting to occupy your mind. The schools here have broken up for the summer recess and Mabel's son Frederick will be arriving in a few days, and next Tuesday he will be going to a commercial college to see if he will be accepted. Otherwise he will have to travel further afield. I suppose they are all men at your place, which I know suits you while you are staying there. While we here in England have been having plenty of rain which they say will probably remain for another three months. Well now, there is little more to add except keep well, my dear, and if there is anything I can do don't hesitate to send your instructions and I will do what I can. Are we allowed to send books, etc? Love as always, Joan.'

Jack now applied the numbers which he always carried in his head. There were thirteen in all and they would be repeated over again according to the length of the letter. He now found the thirty-fifth word was Frederick and the other numbers gave him the message 'Frederick arriving Tuesday commercial travel men's suits staying England three months instructions well to.'

The last two words meant nothing he could put any sense to. They were a continuation of the set of thirteen but in this short letter had no meaning. From the information Jack knew his right-hand man in Germany would be coming to England travelling as a commercial businessman carrying men's suitings. Frederick had benefited very well from their operations and would do all in his power to secure Jack's escape.

The letter was read again, and it was clear that Frederick was now arranging with Joan some of the details; it was up to himself now to reply to his wife so that his escape would be timed for his pick up. He had formulated his plans. It was a matter now of building up

161

sufficient confidence in the prison officers of his ability to perform his duties. As the weeks passed their attention was directed elsewhere as building was in progress at the prison, and he was left to his own devices. Whenever he went fully laden to the pits he would wave to the officer in the tower, who sometimes would respond. But when he returned the officer would not get any sign from him as he sat on the cart looking down in a very dejected attitude, and never looked up at the tower.

That evening Jack again read Joan's letter and realized that the words 'well to' had no meaning but could well have done so had the letter been longer.

The perimeter of the prison compound where the pits were situated was at the edge of a ravine securely separated from the limed pits with barbed wire. The cliffs were over two hundred feet deep.

His escape route would be descending this cliff, and this would require a long coil of strong rope, so that until he could obtain such an item his chances of getting away with time to spare were nil, yet he had to do something so that Joan and Frederick could make their plans before Frederick returned to West Germany.

Where to obtain such a length of rope was his immediate problem, yet once obtained his other plans would hopefully fall into place. In the meantime he had written to Joan using the numbers in a short letter, advising that he had made his plans and would send another letter giving the time and place where he wanted Frederick to be with the car for the journey to Switzerland. He was to obtain the passport and clothing, also he must fix himself up with fishing gear. Jack finished the letter, which looked quite innocuous and passed by the censor after one cursory glance.

Jack knew he would have to steal the rope he required, and once this was reported missing it would create such a tumult that every nook and cranny of the prison would be searched for its recovery; there would be endless searching of the inmates' quarters, who would not feel too kindly disposed to the rope stealer.

From now on Jack kept a watchful eye open, and on his visits to the paint shop where he had to collect his bag of

162

quicklime he had not noticed any rope, until one morning as he was leaving the store he saw a new coil of rope leaning against the wall by the outside door. It had just been delivered while he was in the store and was no doubt required for the scaffolding on the building. The store-keeper, having signed for it, had, for the moment, gone to the other end of the building. Quickly picking it up, Markham rolled it into the back of the cart and laid his two bags of quicklime against it, then taking the rein of the mule led it away faster than the poor animal had moved for years.

His journey to the pits was uninterrupted as the prison officers would keep clear of the liming operation whenever it occurred. Reaching the pits he quickly emptied most of the lime into them before he dug a hole with the spade and buried the coil of rope. Having levelled the ground he next spread dung on the surface and quicklime all around so that it would appear he had made a careless spillage and thrown on the quicklime. When he was satisfied that there was no indication that the ground had been disturbed he completed his usual task of emptying the cart. Then, collecting the mule, returned to the prison buildings seated on the cart, ignoring the watcher on the observation tower as on previous occasions.

Two days' later all convicts were confined to their cells; it was then that he was told by the warden who brought him his food that a coil of rope was missing and every part of the prison would be searched. No prisoner would be allowed to leave his cell until it was discovered. Jack was questioned but they could glean nothing from him. Unknown to him the pits had been inspected but the lime on the ground had forestalled the use of the dogs from approaching close enough to the buried treasure.

Several days passed while the floors and roofs were searched. Each cell was inspected in turn while all bedding was emptied and repacked under the eyes of the officers. The prisoners were in a state of rebellion as the search continued; and it looked extremely unpleasant for the future of the prisoner who had been found to have stolen the rope, not only from the staff but also from the inmates.

It was at this point that a wonderful stroke of luck appeared. A lifer who had manufactured a key to his cell knew that he would have it confiscated, so he took a chance to leave his cell with the key still in the outside lock, which he was able to reach through the bars, and made a completely silent escape. Also, one of the guard dogs was missing. It was therefore assumed he had the rope concealed and had used it to obtain his freedom. The search was now extended to outside the prison, but all to no avail; the prisoner and the dog had vanished. Eventually it was decided to allow the prisoners to resume their normal duties, and Jack welcomed this more than any, for he knew that should the escaped prisoner be captured then the search for the rope would be intensified.

# 15

Joan Markham had been to Bournemouth for the day and it was on her return in the late afternoon that Martha told her there was a letter for her. The stamp denoted the sender, so that as soon as she reached her room she proceeded to read it, with the numbers which she had kept locked in her cabinet.

It was the one she had been praying for, as it gave the date when her husband would be making his bid for freedom. The instructions were very clear as to what he would expect should he get clear of the prison. Joan could hardly wait for Frederick to return from his travels, which she knew would be that evening.

Locking the letter away she went down to the garden and along to the little summer house at the far end where she was able to observe the arrival of cars at the side of the building. When she saw Frederick's draw up near the flower bed she was able to attract his attention. He joined her to hear the news which he said had made his day, for he had been to Winchester where he had to waste his time pretending he was on official business, as he had to do each day to satisfy Martha and the other guests that he was a bonafide trader.

Frederick was as excited as Joan at the news that he could commence work which was in no way fictitious. The late September sunshine was casting shadows into the summer house from the tall trees surrounding the garden as they sat in close proximity discussing the part that Jack required Frederick to play, which was only four days from the date of receiving the letter, so there was no time to lose. Martha rang the dinner bell as the two conspirators completed their arrangements and it was after the meal that Frederick informed Martha that he would be returning to Germany the next morning for some more stock, so he would leave that night as he wished to catch the first boat from Folkestone. His true reason was that he had some telephoning to do, and he had already arranged with the night porter at a hotel overlooking the English Channel to expect him at this late hour.

All went well and Frederick had done his phoning and was pleased with the way the Mercedes was behaving, for he had kept it tuned to perfection for such an eventuality. The crossing was smooth at this early hour and he was able to take a cat nap before disembarking at the port of Boulogne. He collected his car and drove to the outskirts where he telephoned his cousin before the long drive across France to Geneva. There he stayed the night before motoring to Munich, which he reached in the mid-afternoon, completely exhausted.

Having found accommodation at the Central Hotel, he took a hot bath and retired early, sleeping soundly until eight o'clock the next morning when he again motored out to the country which Joan had explained was the point of his hoped-for rendezvous with Jack. The place was by a bridge; Frederick felt if Jack knew of the bridge it would be one near the prison where he was confined, and it was imperative he should find it that day, for tomorrow was the day when, with any luck, he would pick up Jack.

That day he spent going around the countryside as near as he could approach what he felt certain was the prison complex, and having assured himself he was right he then found the nearest bridge downstream from the prison.

Returning to Munich he made a few purchases for one who was going to spend his time fishing the next day, arranging for the hotel to supply plenty of food and drink for a day out.

Jack Markham was feeling the strain of waiting as the time for him to make his bid for freedom approached. The dry harvest weather was continuing. For this he was thankful, for any rain would have washed the quicklime down on to the rope, rendering it useless. The day arrived at last and it proved to be another fine September

166

morning as he looked around his cell for the last time before proceeding to his normal duties, which he hoped never to have to repeat again.

His first action on being let out of his cell was to collect the donkey, but on this occasion his warder preferred to walk along with him, discussing the escape of a prisoner, the object of which was to discover if Jack knew anything about him. In order to get Jack to converse he spoke in a very confidential manner, saying it was strange that one of the dogs had gone missing about the same time. Perhaps he took the dog with him, as he was responsible for looking after the kennels and it seemed he took a liking to one of them.

'You have not noticed anything, I suppose, when you have been collecting?'

But Jack was unable to enlighten him and was pleased, as they approached where the donkey was tethered, that the warder decided there was nothing to be gained and walked away.

With the mule in the shafts the task of emptying, cleaning and loading the cart from the various latrines was accomplished in a more joyful spirit than Jack had experienced for many a day. Even the mule sensed more than the atmosphere and he would turn his head and look at Jack as if he knew the reason for Jack's enthusiasm to complete each task in the shortest possible time. At last all was ready except one more call to the stores for a sack of quicklime, which once aboard, the journey to the pits was made without any obstacles. He gave a cheeky wave to the lone watcher on the tower and was rewarded with seeing the right arm being raised almost as if he was bidding him farewell.

Arriving at the pits he quickly excavated the rope, tying a length to the back of the cart and coiling this around the base of a supporting post nearest the ravine. The mule was then encouraged to move forward, pulling the post out of the ground but without disturbing the electrical wires which ran midway and at the top of the post. He was left sufficient room to crawl underneath and reach the cliff edge, but this was not to be yet, for he had other things to do first.

Divesting himself of his prison garb he draped it over the sack of quicklime which was placed on the driver's seat. Placing his cap on the top of the sack he was able to make it resemble the dejected appearance he always adopted on his return trip. But this time the mule would be pulling a full load, so would be even slower than usual. Untying the rope he secured it to a nearby post and at last crawled under the wire, dragging the rope with him which he tossed over the cliff, hoping it was of sufficient length to reach the bottom of the gully.

The mule, which had not been taken out of the shafts to graze, was quite unperturbed when given the order to gee-up, pulling the cart with the effortless motion at the same slow pace it always adopted. Jack, now clad only in his vest and shorts, started to slide down the rope with the ease he had learnt from his early days in the merchant navy.

The end of the rope lay loose at his feet; there were about twelve feet to spare. Reaching up he sliced through the rope with a knife he had secreted and carried in his mouth as he descended the rope, feeling and looking like some marauding pirate. But his search was not for gold from some stricken ship, but for two planks of wood which he had thrown over the cliff several weeks before and were more precious than any gold. One he saw perched in a low tree and the other on the ground below. The tree loosened its hold of the plank, which Jack soon tied to the other and dragged the short distance to the river.

He entered the water with his raft, gladly having it to hang on to as the cold was so intense that any hope of swimming very far without suffering some form of cramp was a risk he was not prepared to take. As he drifted into deeper water he was gasping for air, as it was as much as he could manage to hang on to the planks. His exertions had warmed him and the icy cold was sapping his strength more than he would have anticipated. The river was flowing fast and in midstream he felt his confidence returning as he became accustomed to the temperature. He was on his way to freedom and he had a good hour before his escape was reported, that is if the guard stationed on the tower accepted his decoy as himself, and the trusty mule walked the journey back at the same unhurried pace which Jack had encouraged it to do.

Frederick was 'fishing' by the bridge when he saw Jack on his planks out in the midstream coming slowly down towards him. When he had arrived within casting distance, Frederick cast his line which had no hook but a lead weight attached on the end. It took two casts before he was able to put it within Jack's reach across the planks where it held fast, fortunately for Jack, who had hardly the strength to hold the line. In no time at all Frederick had pulled him and the raft to the bank, dragging Jack out of the water like a lifeless seal. Jack had lost both his vest and underpants in the struggle to remain with the twisting and turning raft.

Frederick, half lifting and pulling Jack, who being wet and naked he found no easy task, eventually had him bundled on to the back seat of the car and covered with towelling. Then climbing into the driver's seat he set the car in motion to move as quickly as possible in the open country, yet slowing while passing any cottage or village. At one point he stopped and gave Jack brandy. He was recovering and drying himself and felt the blood returning to his feet, which through their being submerged in the cold for such a long period were unable to support him.

Frederick turned to him from time to time and seeing he had sufficiently recovered told him to open the case at the back of the seat where he would find all the clothing he needed. Jack did so and not only discovered every garment fitted perfectly, but in the pocket of the suit he found a wallet with German marks and Swiss franks and a passport for his journey to a land where he would be secure.

At last Jack felt the river had cleansed him of the stench which had been his lot to bear for far too long, and as the miles rolled by and the warmth returned to his frozen limbs, he realized how much he was indebted to Frederick for his part in the escape. Even Jack's jaw which had been stiff with the cold was now loosening, and in order to make conversation he first thanked Frederick, and then asked, 'Why did you push the planks back into the water?'

With his eyes on the road, back came the answer, 'If they found them where you got out of the river, they would have looked for tyre marks and footprints; not many of yours, perhaps, but plenty of my shoe prints. Whereas now the planks which I had no time to untie will be about another five miles down the river, so with luck they will not know you were picked up.'

'Good thinking,' was Jack's only reply.

For the next few miles they remained silent until Frederick said, 'If you lift up the back seat you will find a hamper in there. In its place stuff the wet towels and pass me a sandwich; there's ham and tongue, anything will do. I'm famished and I dare say you will be able to finish them up. We have about 150 miles to go before we reach the Swiss border, and then Zurich where I have booked us up for the night.'

'Will there be any difficulty as we cross the border?'

'Not a bit of it. I shall be crossing at the same spot where I entered Germany because my cousin is a border guard there. Also I have made friends on the Swiss side. You would be surprised what a free shirt or two will accomplish, especially as one is a commercial traveller who can always explain the shirts are discontinued lines. So don't worry. But if anything does happen on the way you get under the back seat and turn the wet towels out.'

Nothing happened to justify this performance, so the entry into Switzerland was accomplished successfully.

Frederick brought the now very dusty Mercedes to a halt at the Imperial Hotel, where a porter who evidently knew Frederick accepted the keys.

Jack and Frederick entered the hotel with the nonchalance of two who had not a care in the world; although Jack still felt strange in his Savile Row suit and good English shoes when only a few hours previously he had been shunned by the very type of men he had once despised.

But now he was prepared to start all over again, living the life to which he had aspired, like a butterfly which had just emerged from the colourless shape of a chrysalis.

Frederick's eyes shone with the success of his endeavours as he remarked to Jack when they had been shown into their apartment, 'I was prepared to have stayed all night, and then every day after for another week if need be.'

Jack could not resist the continental expression of hugging him, but could not accomplish the act with a kiss on either cheek. Disengaging himself with some embarrassment, he turned to the window where there was a small packet on the table. Frederick's voice behind him said, 'There are tickets on the table.'

Picking them up Jack saw they were air tickets for two persons travelling to Tunisia. He turned once more, but only to see Frederick quietly letting himself out of the room, while passing him, with the love-light in her eyes, was his own beloved Joan.

# 16

It had started to rain in London as Nigel Danton left his office near Temple Gardens. The street lights were coming on although it was early in the evening, and by the time he had reached his club the entrance was festooned with cascades of water through which he dashed, to be greeted by the doorman intoning, 'Nasty night, sir.' Nigel made no reply as he shook the raindrops from his coat.

Finding a chair by the fire, which was hardly ever extinguished winter or summer, he received his customary whisky and soda along with the London evening paper, the headlines screaming out, 'Another Escape From West Germany's Top Security Prison.'

Nigel was just about to turn the paper for the latest cricket scores on the back page when the name Jack Markham caught his eye with a more startling effect than the headlines. He read on.

'Another escape has been reported, this time an Englishman serving a term of twelve years for the security van robbery at Hamburg. It would appear he had lowered himself to a watercourse at the edge of the prison compound by means of a rope . . .'

Nigel thoughtfully turned the pages, but his attention was again diverted from the cricket scores by a Stop Press notice on the back page: 'West German prison dog found tied to the railings of a building in the British section of Berlin, along with a cap and a bundle of roughly made clothing from blanket material, but a very good copy of a prison officer's uniform.'

Nigel was considering phoning his friend John at his home in the Cotswolds, to ask if he had heard the news, when the telephone was brought to him. In response to his 'hallo' the secretary George's voice answered, 'I was just about to leave the office when the Commissioner at Scotland Yard phoned to say it was all poppycock about the British keeping an eye open for Markham.

'He said if we see anything in the papers, not to expect to be called to do anything. We're doing damn all about the fellow Markham. He can come and go as far as I'm concerned, and if the Germans want him they can come and look. We are not going to expend any more of our officers' time or money looking for him.'

George concluded, 'The Commissioner sends his regards.'

Nigel smiled, feeling deeply satisfied as he caught the steward's eye that he might have another whisky and at the same time remove the telephone. He was contented as he felt for the card which he had received that morning and kept in his pocket. It was an invitation to a wedding at the home of Lady Ursula Dalsworth.

Lynton Hall was celebrating the marriage of Angela and Clarence when Lady Dalsworth received a message in her private room next to the conservatory. It was a letter brought to her by the maid Rose, who said it had been delivered by hand from a gentleman who said it was urgent. Lady Dalsworth enquired the name of the gentleman, but was told he had not left his name and when asked refused to do so. He had a car with racks in the back on which were men's suits.

Lady Dalsworth opened the letter slowly as she gazed across the park where the villagers were assembling for a firework display, then looking down at the letter she instantly recognised the handwriting.

'Dear Lady Ursula Dalsworth, I wish on behalf of my husband and myself to offer our congratulations and wish Angela and Clarence every happiness, and regret most sincerely our part in causing them so much trouble.

'Jack and I cannot return to England, which we miss so much, but we are safe here and do not want for anything now that we are together . . .'

Lady Dalsworth saw there was more writing but nevertheless smiled as she tore the letter into small pieces before placing it in the wastepaper basket.

She was quite aware from newspaper reports that Jack Markham and his wife Joan were in Tunisia. She was still looking abstractedly across Lynton Park when there was a discreet tap at the door, which was then opened by her son Clarence, accompanied by Angela, who wished to say their goodbyes in private before leaving.

'Thank you, my dears,' was all she could say as they hugged and kissed her. Then recovering herself she said, 'Now we must join the others to give you the traditional send-off; I suppose it is a secret where you are going?'

'Not at all,' replied Angela, 'we shall be at the Hannibal's Palace Hotel on the coast of Tunisia.

Lady Dalsworth's smile was momentarily frozen at this announcement, while the startled look in her eyes was quickly replaced by the customary twinkle, but not unobserved by Clarence.

'You have been reading the papers, mummy.'

'Yes, dear, I have, and it was a surprise to me to know you would be going to the same place where those others were.'

'I know, mother. We had arranged our honeymoon a long time ago, but we shall only be staying a few days as we shall be joining a party sailing along the coast, and then the Greek Islands, before going on to Venice where we shall travel overland to Assisi, then Florence, Rome and Milan.'

Angela interrupted to say, in a jesting voice, 'And Stressa and Lake Maggiore.'

At which Clarence quickly added, 'And the Isle of Beauty; talk about taking coals to Newcastle.'

'That's enough, children.'

'Seriously, mother,' said Clarence, 'we shall keep in touch as we go along, I assure you. Also we will not meet them, or be available should they find out where we are staying.'

'That's all I wanted to hear, my dears, but do take great care.'

Then, addressing them both but smiling at Angela, she said, 'We must not keep your father and the send-off party waiting.'

Nigel Danton and John Royston, having completed the cusomary pranks at the back of the Rolls, joined the assembly to wish the couple goodbye.

Lady Dalsworth, having disposed of her confetti, now stood back as she found her eyes moistening, to cause a mist obscuring the departing carriage. Wiping her eyes she then noticed Angela's father, whose fixed smile was, she felt sure, in contrast to his deeper feelings.

Lady Ursula Dalsworth stepped beside him and took his arm.